Scrooge & Marley:
An Adaptation of Charles Dickens's
A Christmas Carol

Jay R. Swanson

Library of Congress Cataloging-in-Publication Data

Scrooge & Marley An Adaptation of Charles Dickens's
A Christmas Carol / Jay R. Swanson

p. 130. 20.32 cm.

ISBN: 979-8-218-50504-2
eBook ISBN: 979-8-218-51867-7

1. Adaptation of Classic Holiday Fiction 2. LGBTQ
Romance

2024921912

DEDICATION

To everyone who told me to do this,
And everyone, along my way,
Who believed in me.

CONTENTS

Foreword:

As a child, I used to skip these, unless they were part of the assignment. I was certain that if the author wanted this information to be inclusive of the story, they would have, in fact, included it in the story. However, in this case - and please give me the opportunity to surprise you - I could not.

"A Christmas Carol" by Charles Dickens was the first of his works I read. I was in fourth or fifth grade, likely around ten years old. (unsuccessfully, I tried A Tale of Two Cities next but found it a little out of reach). However, "A Christmas Carol" was easy. I had watched many film adaptations; from animated to absurd (highly recommend *Scrooge* from 1975 a musical version with Albert Finney and Alec Guinness, or perhaps *Scrooged* starring Bill Murray) the story was easy to follow.

As much as I love the story, and I love the message of being good to others, there was always a piece of the story that never seemed to fit.

Then I watched a version the television channel FX aired. Dark and macabre, with Guy Pierce as our anti-hero. At one point he laments the death of Jacob Marley. The sorrow in his face and tone snapped into place what I had been missing, what had always bothered me. What was in it for Marley? If they were just business partners, and he was doomed to an eternity in chains, would he offer Scrooge a chance at redemption? Unless they were more intimately involved.

i

In Victorian England, in the 1840s - when the story is set and was written - it was a crime punishable by death for two men to have sexual relations. James Pratt and John Smith were the last two men to be executed for buggery in England[1]. They were hanged on Nov 27th, 1835, outside of the Newgate prison. The man who knew of their relations, William Bonill, was found guilty as an accessory to the crime and sent to Australia, then a penal colony of Great Britain, to live the rest of his natural life. All of their assets went to the crown, Queen Victoria at the time, or "Old Vic" her commoner nickname.

In 1835, years before the publishing of some of his enduring masterpieces and 8 years before writing "A Christmas Carol", Dickens was an unknown journalist. One of his first piece of regular work was a serial originally titled "Sketches by Boz". These were published in a periodical throughout the late 1830s and later collected into an anthology known as The Pickwick Papers. Dickens used these writings to highlight the cruel conditions many people were subjected to in England. One of the accounts titled, "A Visit to Newgate,"[1] chronicled a tour of the famous Newgate Prison in London; the same prison where James Pratt and John Smith were detained.

At a point in the entry, Dickens writes about "two men who had been found guilty of crimes that prevented them from being housed with the other inmates," but doesn't explicitly state which crime.

"No plea could be urged in extenuation of their crime, and they well knew that for them there was no hope in this world...The two short ones,' the turnkey whispered, 'were dead men.'...These two men were executed shortly afterwards." [2]

We know Dickens had sympathy for those less fortunate, those who were cast to the sidelines of society; take for example, his affection for Tiny Tim. Could it be possible Dickens saw the conviction and execution of these men as unjust? As a writer, he may have even concocted a story to save them from the hangman's noose.

They would have to be secretive. They would have to be wealthy enough to secure their privacy and keep everyone they knew at arm's length. Anyone associated was either a witness that could turn them in, or a conspirator that could meet a similar fate. It would be easy to imagine a widower of a secret relationship descending into despair and pushing society and all humanity away, fearing everyone was a potential extortionist.

Dickens wrote the novella "A Christmas Carol" over a six-week period starting in October of 1843[3]. I would feel foolish if I were trying to say that rather than write a Christmas cautionary tale, Dickens intended to tell a story calling for social justice and reform; and yet, isn't that one of the messages from every adaptation and retelling?

Therefore, please consider (and enjoy) my attempt to re-imagine this beloved story to answer a question the original leaves blank.

I am overwhelmed by the many friends and supporters who, on hearing of my idea, told me I must publish, because it was just too good of a concept to let pass; you all have a part to play in this adaptation. I am indebted to my beta-readers: Amber, Becky, Chris, Genay, Greg, Jen, Kathy, Kay, Mei and Patrick. You are my biggest champions. You all created a space in your lives for me and allowed this story to become what it is. I am humbled by your accurate critiques and did my best to use them to improve the story.

I am grateful to editor Will Allison, who provided the most amazing feedback and support. I highly recommend him if you are looking for an editor that just "gets the story" and how to make it better. I also would be lost without the efforts and editing of Genay Jackson; you made this story sound like I knew it could, and I am forever your friend.

I could not and would not forget my own love, Grant. Your care for me and enduring support and, sometimes, directness made this happen. You have taught me how to love and how to be loved. But most of all, you told me that self-forgiveness is a practice and not a one-time thing.

May this story bring you all a sense of peace and love, and as always, God bless us everyone.

References:

1. Old Bailey Proceedings Online (www.oldbaileyonline.org, version
    9.0) September 1835. Trial of JOHN SMITH, JAMES PRATT,
    WILLIAM BONILL (t18350921-1934). Available at:
    https://www.oldbaileyonline.org/record/t18350921-1934
    (Accessed: 21st August 2024).
2. Dickens, Charles. Sketches by Boz. New York, Hurd and
    Houghton, 1867. Pdf. https://www.loc.gov/item/06037036/.
3. The Real Story Behind Charles Dickens' A Christmas Carol
    published Dec. 2020, Available at https//
    https://www.penguin.co.uk/articles/2020/12/charles-dickens-a-
    christmas-carol-story-of (Accessed 21st August of 2024).

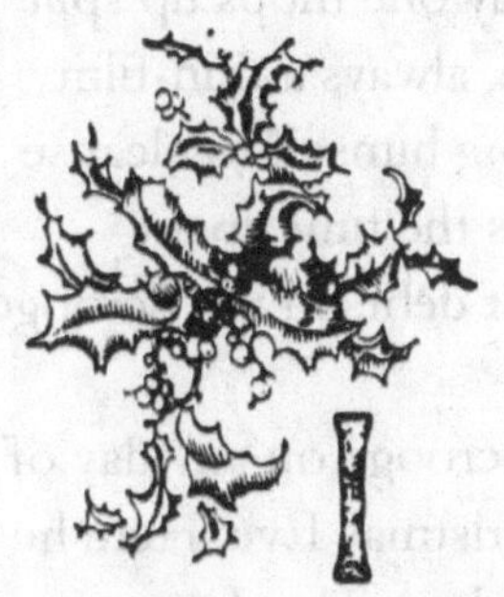

I

MARLEY'S RETURN

Just as it has always been stated at the beginning, Jacob Marley was dead. And, had been so for the past seven Christmas seasons. Leaving no doubt, there was no life in him; in one that had previously been so full of it. In his passing, he had left his finances to his business partner, executor, and sole friend, Ebeneezer Scrooge.

The inseparable and determined Scrooge and Marley, always searching for their next business deal. Yet, one really had to be on his last penny before even considering gracing the door of their counting house. Not known for generous money lending, but rather, crafting deals with impossible terms. Most other lenders and business owners were in awe of Scrooge and Marley's success, while privately they shook their heads at how the two preyed on the most despondent of borrowers.

1

It was in this way they had maintained a handsomely profitable business and a network of anxious indebted Londoners. It wasn't only, in this way, Scrooge and Marley were bound.

Scrooge tried to blot the memory of Marley's death from his waking moments the way one mops up spilt milk. He wavered in his diligence, always a thin-film residual he could never really bring himself to cleanse completely. His only reprieve was the time spent pouring over his cataloged lists of debts in the Scrooge and Marley Counting House.

This is where one can find Scrooge on any day of the calendar, including today, Christmas Eve. Here he is, sullen and hunched over his ledger. The deep furrows in his brow and the creases around his eyes making his face more like a shadow in the dim candlelight; slowly collapsing into the hollowness left by Marley's absence. Finding he much preferred the cheap comfort of cold and austerity to the happiness of others. The cold, it seemed, frightened away the despair of emptiness, or at least it was friends with it. A small scratching sound and throat clearing from the doorway was just enough to arouse his attention, but he kept his eyes trained downward on his meticulous calculations.

"It's closing time, Mr. Scrooge." Despite the frigid office and interactions with Scrooge, their employee, Bob Cratchit, remained. Bob spoke in a timid voice frozen to the threshold of the office previously occupied by both employers. An empty leather office chair, dust covered and exactly where its prior master had left it, watched on as Scrooge continued scribbling in his ledger under the dismal light of the solitary candle, which cast shadows deepening the wrinkles and folds of his scowl. "Correct, Cratchit."

Bob gripped his second-hand top hat and cleared his throat. "And being as tomorrow is Christmas, sir, I was hoping to spend the whole day with my family."

Scrooge lifted his quill and placed it reverently in its stand. "The whole day." One eye cocked up, still avoiding looking directly at his employee.

Bob wrung his hands along the brim of his hat. "If it's convenient, sir."

Something in his timid clerk's response resurrected a memory from Scrooge's past: *a smiling Jacob Marley standing in the doorway of his parents' home, opening the manor, welcoming in Scrooge. "You should stay the night. If it's convenient?"*

Coming back to himself, Scrooge shook his head. "No, Cratchit. It is not." Scrooge closed the ledger. "But maybe a day without your interruptions and incompetence would be welcome." He sneered. "Take the day." Scrooge dismissed him with the wave of a hand that would have backhanded the man were he standing closer.

Bob hurried to leave before Scrooge could change his mind. He blew out the candle on his desk and reached for the front door. In a moment of happiness for the time off, Cratchit turned back. "Merry Christmas, Mr. Scrooge."

Scrooge looked directly into the eyes of his only employee. "Humbug," he growled as Cratchit withdrew.

As quickly as the door closed, it flew open.

Scrooge expected Cratchit had forgotten something but instead found himself looking upon the genial face of his only living blood relative.

"A Merry Christmas to you, uncle. God save you." His nephew Fred, festively dressed and bundled against the cold, produced a wreath of holly with a leaf of mistletoe swinging on a red ribbon in the center.

A sideways leer crept across Scrooge's face, he harrumphed at the intrusive younger man and stood, carrying his ledger to the safe behind him. "What do you want?"

Fred cleared his throat, coughing into his hand and then blowing on it. "You could keep a warmer business if you wanted more of it. Or are you worried you will melt more than an asset?"

Scrooge regarded his nephew, "How now? You've come to mock me, in my own office during business hours?"

Still smiling, Fred replied, "Business hours? This late on Christmas Eve? I'm surprised you have any business to do, everyone else bunked off after lunch. It's as if you delight in finding ways to make yourself more miserable."

Scrooge tried to be angry with his nephew, but it was moments like this he was reminded of the affection he had always felt for the young man. "It's a wonder you made it into any career other than politics. You're quite the persuasive one."

"It was said, so was my mother." Fred's expression faltered briefly as he mentioned his mother before returning to its genial expression. He proffered the wreath, mistletoe swinging again. "For you."

Scrooge observed the gift, seeing a different memory yet attached to the one from before: *mistletoe suspended in the Marley manor foyer. Scrooge stopping to look up at it as the front door closed behind him. Marley chuckling, helping Scrooge remove his coat. "Standing under that will only get us in trouble Eb."* Scrooge realized he had closed his eyes when his nephew's voice drew him out of the memory.

"I see maybe I have persuaded you," Fred exclaimed. The corners of Scrooges mouth had turned awkwardly upward with a cracking of his jaw, popping as it moved in an unfamiliar direction. "Dine with me and my wife Clara tomorrow. It's a day for family." Fred hung the wreath on the knob of Scrooge's office door. "It's what mum would've wanted."

Scrooge didn't often think of his sister, but he couldn't help seeing her compassion and her strength in her son's eyes. It was his love for his sister and her son that weakened, but also hardened his conviction to keep shunning away his family.

"I must close up." Scrooge grabbed a coin purse off his desk and secured it into the safe behind him.

His nephew's smile melted away. "I hope you reconsider coming tomorrow." He returned his top hat to his head with a tap. "You would be welcome to my home on any day, but particularly tomorrow."

While it was difficult for Scrooge to not be suspicious of everyone, he was tempted to offer his nephew the benefit of the doubt. At the same time, he realized no one was ever this pleased to see him, at least not anymore. Turning back, Scrooge busied himself with a stack of papers he wasn't actually reading, until he heard the main office door close. He looked over the top of his glasses to confirm he was blessedly alone again, blowing out a big exhale as he collapsed into his chair. The gust of breath carried the top sheet of paper toward the empty, dust-covered desk that mirrored his own. Scrooge stood quickly, snatching the paper back.

Something, like a whisper, echoed through the dark, from the front office, from behind him, from the corners of the room, from all around him. "Eb?"

The nickname only one person ever called him. Though he was certain he had earned plenty of other nicknames he was content to remain ignorant of.

He paused for a moment, stricken, before convincing himself it must have been the sound of wind under the door or swishing through a window that wasn't closed well enough. Scrooge hurried into his overcoat and finally extinguished the lone candle at his desk on his way to exit.

Once safely outside he locked the door but remained staring at it. "Ghosts," Scrooge muttered to himself, as turned to go home. In his haste, he collided with a huddled figure trying to push past him.

"Eh. Wasat." It was the widow Mrs. Dilber, come to clean the office for the day. Scrooge let her work to pay off the debt her late husband owed. It had been long enough that the original debt was sorted, but along the way Mrs. Dilber found it difficult to keep up with expenses of her own. Scrooge had offered other loans with the expectation of her continued services. There wasn't enough cleaning in all of London for her to work off what she owed now.

"Ah." Scrooge regarded the woman with a distaste he only slightly cared if she saw before distancing himself from her.

"Oh, Sir." She clasped her hands, imploring, closing the distance between them once again. "Being it's Christmas and all, maybe I ken clean d'office a day affa tomorra'? Misser. Cratchit jus tole me you be takin' the day. And I alrea' done the 'ouse and sent ya' linens ta' laundress."

Scrooge's lips curled into a sly smile. "You know, once in my life I had been keenly aware of the magic of Christmas, Mrs. Dilber." Her face brightened as hope became a glimmer of reality. "But I never knew it was so amazing that the dirt and dust from a day of coal fire weren't allowed to collect in its presence."

Her face slid back into its normal dissatisfied look, dropping her hands. "It han't been magic 'ince Misser Marley die'." A knowing smile crept across her face, rotted tooth showing as she opened the door to the dark office. "Ya knew I's commin'. You coulda left a candle lit. It's dark as a grave in'ere."

Scrooge gave Mrs. Dilber a curt nod and turned to be on his way. He effortlessly wove through the crowd of "Happy Christmas" well-wishers making their way home from work and errands. Many passersby recognized the miser, going at great lengths to leap out of his way, or turn from him. It was how Scrooge preferred it; no one stopped to ask what direction the park was, no child asked for the time, no beggar for a coin.

He was intent on reaching his home, the building he and Marley owned and now was just his. A building with six apartments, only two ever occupied and now just one. Nothing was wrong with the building. The walls met the floors, the windows opened, and the fireplaces were clean. Scrooge reasoned, nodding his head, it was certainly not a place for disembodied voices to concern him, it was more proper than that.

"Mr. Scrooge. A moment of your time." A familiar and unwelcome voice interrupted Scrooge in his thoughts. It was Charles Darcy, a colleague from the Exchange and a long-time friend of Marley's.

"No." Scrooge pulled his coat tighter as a winter gust threatened to blow off his hat. People around him cackled and hooted at the winds attempt to dampen their Christmas spirit.

Darcy chuckled and Scrooge seethed. "Come now Scrooge," Darcy chortled. "It's Christmas? Let us get a drink, and we can discuss the charitable contributions you've made to my foundation for the poor this year."

"My good sir! I would be quite surprised to learn there have been any charitable contributions made in my name." Scrooge spat over his shoulder, pushing past the man.

"As would anyone." Darcy didn't follow as Scrooge picked up his pace, testing his luck in the snow and ice. "It's been more than seven years since your last. You can't remain tucked in your own world forever, solitary as an oyster. Someday you're going to need someone else now that..."

Scrooge turned a corner and, blessedly, no longer heard the man.

After the events of the evening, he felt immense relief seeing his three-story apartment building. The sturdy wood of the door stained dark to match the shutters of the upper levels. The hinges were silent in their work and kept the door closed tight, no drafts between frame or threshold. The lion-faced knocker in the center, to Scrooge's knowledge, had not been used in the entirety of his residency. He normally gave it no extra thought, except tonight, it was supporting a pile of snow, giving rise to yet another long-buried memory.

"Get that blunderbuss over there." A kneeling Jacob Marley pointed at a man dodging behind the carriage house. Scrooge launched a snowball, just missing the runner's leg. "Oh, good shot chap, you almost got him."

Scrooge was a guest at the Marley family Christmas celebration. He was not aware that he would be engaged in a bragging-rights-for-a-year snowball fight with Marley's cousins from Devonshire. They, at least, were mostly protected behind a wall of snow Marley had piled up earlier in preparation for the melee.

Suddenly, all three of Marley's cousins careened from the side of the building, running in between the winter dormant bushes and hedge. The men growled as more snowballs were loosed across the garden. Marley and Scrooge crouched together to keep from exposing any part of themselves to the enemy; leg touching leg, shoulder to shoulder, breath panting in unison.

Marley looked down at their half a dozen balls of snow. "I think we're done for." He smirked at Scrooge.

"Follow my lead." Scrooge stood with arms stretched overhead. "I yield."

The cousins stopped mid- attack. "There's no yielding," one yelled as he hurled a ball at Scrooge, just missing his midsection.

In the moment of surprise, Marley popped up and threw the rest of the snowballs, striking all three men in quick succession.

"Hah-hah!" Marley punched the sky in triumph.

"We win!" said Scrooge as the two embraced and tumbled back into the makeshift fort.

Frozen and breathless, Marley and Scrooge laid on their backs laughing themselves to tears while the defeated cousins threw what snowballs remained at them.

The memory faded as Scrooge blinked snow from his eyelashes which was now causing his vision to blur. He brushed the top of the knocker clean and opened the door.

"Eb."

There it was, the same whispered voice as before. Or, was it just the scratching of the key in the lock? Scrooge purposefully averted his eyes from the knocker as he turned the key, as it appeared to have transformed with the removal of the snow and now more resembled a man's face than a lion's. Scrooge didn't linger and closed the door with a slam.

"There," he exhaled, locking the door. He would have lied had anyone asked if he were frightened. He made a life of lies and was good at it, perhaps most especially good at lying to himself.

Trying to relax into his routine, Scrooge bent to the small table in the entry, to light a half-melted tapered candle. The meager light actually seemed to worsen the shadows. And, not at all because his name was whispered by an ethereal voice, but naturally to double check Mrs. Dilber's housework, did Scrooge take more care than usual to investigate the vacant rooms of his building.

He made his residence in one of the third-floor apartments, previously in the name of Jacob Marley. Scrooge found it more comforting than the unit across the hall that had been registered in his name, likely because he had never slept there even one night. It had been made up to look like he lived there, or at least someone lived there. It now contained some of Marley's beloved belongings Scrooge couldn't look at or get rid of; boxed and solidly stocked away, providing no influence on his emotions from in their wooden coffins.

Starting at the first floor, Scrooge jiggled each knob, pressed each door firmly. Ascending to the second floor to do the same, arriving at the same conclusion: no one appeared to be present except himself or perhaps a rodent mistakenly looking for food or respite in this building.

Satisfied - and feeling a bit foolish - he returned to the spiral grand stair at the front of the building with its worn wooden steps. Scrooge knew to walk close to the wall on a particular step between the second and third floor that otherwise would produce a death-raking screech through the stairwell. Marley, however, loved the sound and would sometimes stop on the step to accentuate the creaking echo. He said it did the old building good to hear itself. Scrooge disagreed and took great care to avoid the step and the noise.

Approaching his apartment, Scrooge was now convinced the events from his office and the front door had been a figment of his imagination, brought on by hunger. Quickly, he closed the door and engaged all three locks.

But as he turned to the room and began to remove his overcoat, he heard the shriek of the stairstep he always avoided. He settled his nerves by assuring himself it was merely the stairs shuddering in protest, as he had not only outwitted them on this ascent but had been able to avoid the blood-freezing sound for as many ascents and descents as he could recall.

Scrooge busied himself to drown out the worry growing in his chest. He lit the fire but kept it small, he didn't need a big fire for the meager meal of broth and hard roll. Even more meager than usual, finding he had no appetite again, just wanted to get to bed. He intended to get to the office early before anyone could remind him what day it was, continuing his best to ignore it.

Scrooge went to his bedchamber to secure himself into his evening attire. Again, a sound, a scraping, outside of his bedchamber door. This sound, he reasoned, was a bird resting over the chimney top to absorb some of the warmth, even from the meager diner fire. But it sounded more like it had come from the sitting room he was about to enter.

"Eb."

He was out of alternate explanations now. Someone was in his rooms.

"I am armed and have the law on my side. You are trespassing. What happens to you at my hand the law will see as just." Scrooge was able to hold back from his voice the pounding his heart was making in his chest. He crept along the wall until he could see around the door into the sitting room. The fire and the candle he brought in had gone out, plunging the room into darkness. Only the curtain-filtered moonlight provided any illumination of the room.

Enough light to see near the fireplace, in one of the two green wingbacks, hovered an enigmatic aura. Scrooge couldn't keep himself from investigating. He moved two long-steps before halting. The armchair with the light had not sat an occupant for seven years. However, it was now occupied by a man of greenish hue, dressed in an unkempt suit littered with motheaten holes and covered in cobwebs.

"Do you not recognize me, Eb? Has it been so long?"

Scrooge's heart pounded faster at the sound. A voice he believed he would never hear again. A voice he knew very well indeed, coming from the mouth of a man he would never forget. "Jacob."

Marley nodded, "You must be surprised to see me."

Scrooge forced a scowl, drawing from his armory of tactics to fend off how frightened the moment was making him. "No, I am not. You are always distracting my mind. And it's as if I have pushed you aside too many times, and like that squeaky floorboard on the stair, I am being overruled in my sanity and thus have manifested you in my living quarters."

Marley maintained a serene face, though he too was nervous to be able to talk with Scrooge. He had to be firm with him, which he wasn't ever good at. How he wished to tell him everything straight away, but he needed to be practical. Scrooge would listen only once he could believe what he was seeing.

"You always struggled to accept the magic of the world." Marley tutted and shook his head, as a small smile appeared on his gaunt visage. "Well then, perhaps you are right. I may just be a hunger hallucination." The spirit of Jacob Marley folded his arms, placing both feet down on the floor. "You have been starving yourself of many things, Eb."

The spirit stood. For the first time Scrooge noticed a long, thick chain wound around the man's arms, torso, and legs. The irons clanked as he moved, unwinding from around the chair, trailing behind like a bride's veil. The awful clatter on the wood floor reverberated through the room. Scrooge was sure anyone walking down the street below would wonder what could he be doing this late at night.

Scrooge shrank away from the specter, placing one hand in front of him as if to stop the advancing spirit.

"Eb." Marley halted. "You have no reason, nor will you ever, have a reason to fear me."

Scrooge stood taller and dropped his arms. "I know you are right." Scrooge sighed. "And yet I don't believe this is happening."

"Trust me as you once did." Marley smiled, extending an open palm to him. "I come to warn you, to beg you." His smile stretched to concern; his brow furrowed. "A touch of my hand and you will feel the weight of the burden I carry."

Scrooge was hesitant but wanted to trust Marley, wanted to believe what he was seeing. "Why tonight of all nights? It's been seven years Jacob." Scrooge looked at Marley's outstretched hand but struggled to reach forward and touch him.

Marley smiled yet again, dust dancing off his cheeks as he inclined his head towards Scrooge. "You and I share a bond, a vow we took between us in the secret of this room." Marley looked around and Scrooge relaxed a little; for only the real Jacob Marley would know what they had between them. "You wouldn't forget, we first met forty years ago on this night, and I promised we would have as many Christmases together."

Scrooge's vision blurred, likely an effect of the darkness and not an emotion from remembering Marley's promise. "Aye." His voice shaky and barely a whisper; he would never forget that day.

"And I have kept my promise. I don't know if it will console you a little or haunt you more," Marley looked sorrowful as he spoke, "but I have sat in this chair across from you many nights. Wishing you would hear my plea. I cannot explain why tonight you hear and see me, other than the magic of a lovers promise kept on our anniversary. Or, I desperately needed you to hear me this time." Marley again offered his open palm forward, beckoning Scrooge to touch him.

Scrooge wasn't sure he was comforted, but he had often felt Marley's presence. "Then you heard me talking to you." He placed his hand on top of the spectral image's and felt a tingling in his palm that hummed through his arm and straight to his heart. The feeling softened his demeanor. "At least I can see and hear you now, even if I can't understand how."

Marley nodded, bowing, fetters shaking as they rose into the air a few inches hoisted by the chains. Scrooge's mouth went dry as he suddenly found himself levitating as well.

The humming of warmth, initially pleasant, was now cold and heavy; the weight of the chains wrapping around, pressing in on him. He felt the sadness and a pain he couldn't describe, a feeling so heavy he was moved to a scream.

"Jacob, what is this?" he cried, his open hand covering his face. "I cannot bear it."

"I am sorry, Eb. I wish you had really heard me before this night." The lines of worry on Marley's forehead deepened. "The chains are made from decisions we make in our lives and are then bestowed on us after death. Each link representing an injustice we caused or an unreasonableness we could have prevented, had we only been kinder to our fellow man."

"Does everyone have such long and heavy chains?" Scrooge winced, the pain intensifying. "Jacob, you were as kind as my sister."

"Only someone who loves me as much as you, would think I was kind." He gestured to the unfurling seemingly infinite strand of links. "These are our chains, Eb; grown more terrible and heavier since my death."

"Our chains, Jacob? I don't understand." Scrooge found the pain so unbearable he was gasping through gritted teeth. "Speak comfort to me."

Marley couldn't put Scrooge through the agony associated with the chains any longer and released the man. Scrooge immediately dropped to the floor, landing with a thump on his backside. The pain of the landing a relief to what the chains had been causing him.

Marley seemed to rebound, rising higher. "Earthly vows do not end at death." Marley sighed. "I carry them willingly for the love I share with you. I have no regret from our life." Marely squinted and grunted again. "These chains are not made because of who we were to each other, but because we lacked that same kindness or generosity with others."

Scrooge felt anger rise in him. "But were they generous and kind to us, Jacob? Did they let me have anything to remember you by except this building and our business, both which were legally mine anyway?" Scrooge found strength to stand. "Would they have let us be as we were in these rooms outside? I wasn't even allowed to attend your funeral."

"All people have some chains at the end of their existence, Eb," Marley continued levitating, the chains drawn taut beginning to twist and pull at the spirit's body. "All will answer for their actions, as we have and will for ours."

Scrooge, forgetting the pain of the chains, started to shake in frustration. "I know you always said things to help me see more gratitude in the world. But," Scrooge spluttered. "It was everyone outside of these walls who conspired against us. Somehow you always seemed to ignore it, but I couldn't." The many years since Marley's death had only compounded the ferocity Scrooge used in his money dealings. "And I know we lived safer for the ways we conducted our business."

Marley raised a finger, hushing Scrooge. "Eb, I agree. The more money we could make the safer we were. But it wasn't at the expense of anyone we knew. The many who lost their jobs and livelihoods; the poor and destitute we disregarded without a second thought."

Scrooge's eyes widened, throwing his hands in the air. "Jacob! It kept us safe, bought the building so no one else could live here, hired indebted staff that feared our wrath so they would avoid us as much as possible." Scrooge halted in his litany of ways they had altered their lives, "we even kept family away." Upon saying this, he finally realized that he had been refusing to resign any of his anger at the world for forcing them to live how they had and what he had to endure after Marley's death.

Scrooge looked up at the suspended ghost hoping for a response to the justification, watching the chains tighten their grip as Marley grunted and grimaced. "Again, you are right. We couldn't have been as we would've liked outside of this room. And we made all our decisions together. But now, I see we shouldn't have disregarded others, for fear of the way we would have been treated."

Scrooge made to answer, fire back another time they were almost discovered, how they could have been extorted, or worse, sent to the gallows. However, something in the way Marley looked at him halted his response.

Marley was clearly in exquisite pain. Scrooge had only experienced it for a brief moment. An eternity of unrest was difficult for Scrooge to grasp, he swallowed and cleared his throat, "So, what's to become of us now, Jacob?"

Marley exhaled a groan. "It is up to you Eb, to help us both. If you do not do what you can to reverse the hold these chains have, we will be doomed to wander the afterlife with them, never achieving a restful sleep.

Never to enjoy an eternity in peace."

Scrooge sniffed, wiping his nose with the back of his hand. He disregarded the odd feeling of wetness in his eyes. "What can I do? I'm not good at life, not without you."

The chains tightened, pulling at Marley, the ends vanishing as they continued to hoist him through the air and seemingly into the ceiling. "You will be visited by three ghosts, starting at midnight tonight. They will remind you about your past, show you what you will miss out on in the present, and what may be should you remain unchanged." Marley's back was against the ceiling.

"Please don't leave me again," Scrooge implored on bent knees. "It's been so wretched without you."

Marley's eyes cataracted and his features hollowed, his face ashen, his wavy brown hair thin and bleached. "Heed their lessons and perhaps what is foretold can be changed, and we may once again be happily together."

Marley's ghost disappeared through the rough plaster ceiling, leaving no trace. Scrooge blinked the room into focus, wiping his eyes; the fire was again burning low, the candle lit, the door was closed and triple locked, everything was as he had left it.

Scrooge was horrified, shaking, unsure of what to do with himself. No longer interested in eating, he tried to sit in his wingback chair, but it faced the one Marley had been sitting in, and it bothered him to consider what had transpired.

The clock on the otherwise empty mantel chimed ten o'clock.

Scrooge looked at the hour to confirm the strokes of the bell. "But that's not possible. I only just got home." The whole encounter must have lasted longer than he thought.

He was trembling. The cold, maybe? "But it couldn't have been real." Scrooge looked up at the ceiling where Marley had been lifted and then, taking the candle in hand, inspected the green wingback chair he never sat in, but was always sure to keep clean. Discovering that there was no change to it—exactly what he expected—Scrooge took himself to bed.

THE PAST

Scrooge was in the process of closing the bed curtains as the clock in the living room rang eleven. It had scarcely been minutes since it rang ten.

"Humbug," Scrooge yelled back at it.

To which the clock responded by chiming midnight.

He froze. The church bell across the square rang the midnight hour as well. Scrooge wrapped into his dressing gown tighter and placed a stocking cap on his head. He now felt absolutely certain he was losing his faculties as a light appeared in the center of his room.

"What's this now?" Scrooge demanded. His heart skipped a beat, hoping for a moment that it might be Marley returning. Or, was this to be one of the others he warned of? The light formed, a wispy pulsating glow around a central orb, and flashed a white brilliance before coalescing.

"Are you the spirit Jacob told me would come?" Scrooge squinted, unable to see in the brightness.

"I am." The voice came from the orb, but it seemed like he heard it in his head. It was a louder sound than he thought a light could make, and yet it was also softer, more soothing than he expected. What was not at all soothing however, was its brightness.

Scrooge raised a hand to protect his eyes; blinded, he continued to squint, looking down and away. He was not afraid of a ball of light – he was a man of reason after all – but this was beyond comprehension.

The light spoke in his mind again. "You appear apprehensive of me."

Scrooge shook his head with a vehemence, almost to convince himself. "No, spirit. It is just that you are so bright, I cannot look at you without fearing I'll go blind."

The light dimmed, Scrooge observed the orb wasn't just light, but rather a floating firefly—no, a floating tiny being with wings—no, something else. Scrooge gaped. A wood sprite or will'o-the-wisp, he may have heard his mother describe them when he was a child.

"No need to stare."

Scrooge felt a turn of his mouth, painful and awkward, into a half grin. "Forgive me spirit. But, it's just, now that I see you, I don't know what to call you."

"Regardless of what you would want to call me, I am the Ghost of Christmas Past." Putting hands to hips, the tiny sprite struck a mighty proud pose. "Specifically, your Christmas past."

"And why, dear spirit, might I have need to discuss such?" Scrooge thought Marley was warning him about their future.

"We shall see. Here." The spirit extended a hand. "Come closer."

Scrooge started to but halted, recalling that wood sprites were mischievous, and his mother had warned him not to negotiate with them or enter into any contract. Merely doing as they asked could be considered submission, and then one would fall under their spell.

"There is no reason to fear," the spirit said. "Besides, you have yet to really believe any of this is happening...haven't you?"

Scrooge agreed, and yet, he did feel something had started to change. The emotions inside him, as soon as he saw Marley, but maybe more, allowing himself to remember the way they were when Marley was alive. Even if this was a dream or a hallucination, he needed to understand better what he could do for them both. He crouched down closer to the little being.

The Ghost of Christmas Past brought a closed fist to its mouth, with the thumb side closest to its lips, as if to cover a cough. As Scrooge watched, the ghost blew a gust of air into the closed hand. As the spirit's hand opened, Scrooge was assaulted with a barely detectable glittery substance that danced upon his eyelashes and lips. It made him feel a little giddy, and he laughed a surprised sound, like a drunk after a hiccup.

The spirit smiled. "You'll now be able to see the past as I see it. But you must do what I say." The spirit once again stretched an open palm toward Scrooge.

"Touch my hand, and we will see what we can find."

Scrooge touched the tip of his index finger to the spirit's palm and felt a warmth emanating out from the center of his body. It spread toward his feet, hands, and head, but rather than consuming him, burning him alive, the heat swaddled him, enveloped him, and his apartment vanished around him.

The next thing he knew, it was a bright day in the countryside. In front of him stood the gate to his old boarding school, a loathsome and wretched place where he had learned a lot about rejection and how to fend for himself.

"Spirit, why bring me to this despicable place? There was never a good memory here." Scrooge's frown had returned, deepening his sharp features. His body was rigid as the spirit pulled him forward.

"Nevertheless," the spirit said, "Christmas time comes here too." They entered the schoolyard, bustling with activity as adults and children mingled, throwing arms around each other. "And fear not, these beings only exist in your memory. They are not aware of our presence." They passed many horse-drawn carriages filled with belongings and families ready to head home for a festive winter celebration. "Look at how much joy and love abounds!" The spirit smiled, floating along at Scrooge's eye level.

Scrooge regarded the chaos with the same hardened expression. "Not for me."

The spirit nodded. "The school hasn't completely emptied yet, has it?"

Instantly the scene dissolved into a dormitory room, a young boy sitting on a made-up cot, dressed for travel, luggage at his feet.

Two other boys ran past him. "They aren't coming for you, Sneezer!"

"Yeah, no one wants you," the other shouted as they collapsed on each other in a fit of laughter. "You're too weird. No one knows what to do with you."

"Children can be so cruel," the Ghost of Christmas Past tsked.

Scrooge nodded. "What hurt the most was the truth of their ridicule. This must be my first year here, I knew better than to even get ready in the Christmases of the following years." The old man hung his head, eyes closed.

"But why?" the spirit asked with caring sincerity.

Scrooge shook his head. "I reasoned it wasn't practical for my parents to travel by coach to get me and then have to cover my costs at the boarding school while I wasn't there. I was an investment for my family, and I knew my place." Scrooge looked down on his younger self. "My father was not a kind person. He believed this school would make me a 'true man'. Since his belt couldn't." Scrooge cleared his throat, remembering the lashings he endured at his father's drunken tirades. "He knew I was different."

"Though he did have you home one year, no?" The spirit regarded its charge as the memory dawned on Scrooge.

They were in the same room, but this time they observed a few-years-older Scrooge now laying on his stomach, legs bent up as he read a thick volume, unaware a young woman had entered the room.

"Brother? Dear Ebby."

The boy jerked up. "Fan? Is that you?"

A fair-faced girl with dark curly hair, a few years older than Scrooge, hurried towards him. "Dear brother. I have come to bring you home. I finally convinced father, something in him has changed and he is much kinder now. He ordered a coach and sent me to collect you. We are to be together all Christmas long!"

The young man jumped up and embraced his sister. "I will only believe it because you are telling me so. How ever did you convince him?"

She only offered a demure closed mouth smile, not answering his question. "Go. Get your things, the cab is waiting."

"Even as delicate of a creature she was, her strength is admirable," the spirit remarked as it watched the scene, gently floating to-and-fro, over Scrooge's right shoulder.

"I will not deny it." Scrooge moved out of the way of his younger self running past to take his sister's hand on his way out of the room. "She was exceptionally smart too. And had a way of making me feel special and wanted." Scrooge's lip turned up to a wry smile, coming a little easier this time.

The room started to darken. "Then let us see another Christmas with her."

Scrooge's face dropped in horror. "Oh, please spirit, not that day."

The room dissolved into a parlor room. Scrooge recalled it to be the apartment in which his sister and brother-in-law lived. "Why show me this?" he asked.

The spirit put a finger to its lips, quieting him.

A man he knew as Bentley, his sister's husband, sat on a wooden chair in the corner seemingly unaware of the young child playing quietly at his feet. The man looked as though he'd been pulled apart and put back together haphazardly, his hair unkempt and his clothing soiled with crumbs and drink. Scrooge watched as a younger him – this one in his mid-twenties, a dashing and strong-backed, broad-shouldered version of himself he forgot ever existed – entered the room. "Bentley. You cannot carry on like this. They need you."

The young lad, seeing his uncle, jumped up and ran to hug his legs. Young Scrooge bent down, smiling, and rubbed the child's hair. "Happy Christmas, Fred." Scrooge presented a small package to the boy, which he snatched up eagerly and started to shake.

"Lucie," Bentley slurred. "Take Fred away." The nanny entered the room and with a look of sadness, took the child by the hand. Fred protested but complied and waved to Scrooge on his way out.

"What do you know of need? You have no child. No wife." His brother-in-law rebuffed Scrooge's admonishment with the wave of a hand and a look of disgust as he stood. "What brings you?" Bentley reminded him of his and Fan's late father, red-faced and stumbling as he looked on the verge of being sick.

Scrooge straightened his waistcoat and stood tall. "It's Christmas. A time for family."

"Family?" The man looked gravely at his tumbler glass of dark liquid comfort. "Humbug."

Scrooge watched the interaction, mouth open in wonder. Reliving it, thawing many of his frozen emotions.

"You don't have to do this alone." Young Scrooge put his arms out towards the man, searching for an embrace. "Please. You're the only family I'll have left."

The older man scoffed and sneered, gesturing to the bedchamber door. "Know this. After she's gone, you're no family of mine." He pushed past Scrooge, avoiding his outstretched arms.

Scrooge and the spirit watched as his younger self hung his head and walked to the door of his sister's chamber. He knocked and entered the adjoining room, and Scrooge and the ghost followed. The shades were drawn and the fire roared. Scrooge recalled the room had been so hot, and yet his sister had been so chilled, shaking in her bed.

"Spirit! I cannot watch this. Please, take me from here."

Placing finger to lips again, the spirit responded, "You need to remember."

Scrooge stepped back to watch his younger self talk to his sister, knowing now it would be just hours before she would perish.

"Fan?" his younger self uttered from the doorway.

"It's so cold in here." Her lips chattered. "Come closer, my brother, and bring me some warmth."

Young Ebeneezer pulled a quilt over his shivering sister. He removed his jacket and placed that on her too. "There."

She smiled and appeared to relax just a bit. "Happy Christmas, Ebby."

"Happy Christmas, Fan." Scrooge knelt on the floor beside her. She reached out a hand and he took it. "When you get better and are out of this bed, we can have fun like we did as children. We can play games just like we did when you brought me home from school that year."

Fan smiled, eyes closed before she squinted some and furrowed her brow. "Yes. Just like when we were kids." She coughed into the quilts wrapped around her neck before relaxing again.

"Or maybe," he leaned forward, "We could sing songs. Like the ones we sang on the way back to the boarding school."

Fan appeared to consider this memory. "Why would you want to remember school, Ebby? I know it wasn't easy for you."

Young Scrooge reclined back on his heels, sitting away from her. "I did my best."

"That's not what I mean." She coughed. "You were a great student. And your apprenticeship now is a testament to that."

"I am trying to do the family proud."

His sister opened her eyes and squeezed his hand tighter. "You have always made me proud. You won't ever forget that, will you?"

"Never, Fan." Tears formed in the young man's eyes. The spirit watched as Scrooge wiped the back of his sleeve on his face, muttering something about the late hour and having old eyes that could no longer see with only the dark light of the fireplace.

Young Scrooge continued, "It's only a matter of time now, before I move to the Exchange. Mr. Fezziwig has assured me I have what it takes to represent him well. I just need the right moment to prove myself. Show him I can handle negotiations like businessmen."

"You will, dear brother. I have no doubt. You are
gifted at reading people." Fan lapsed into more
coughing. Eventually she continued. "It's what we both
learned as children."

He nodded, bowing his head, hiding the tears from
his sister at her reference to how they survived their
childhood together.

Scrooge watched on from the other side of the bed
and was startled to notice the blood on her bed linens
after her coughing fit.

"I must ask you to promise me something." Her
eyes opened, distant but bright, meeting her brother's
patient and willing ones.

"Anything for you, Fan." He gripped her hand
tighter.

She smiled and squeezed his back. "You must learn
to forgive yourself for who you are. I see you trying to
fit in, but I know there is something you're missing. I
hope you find it."

Young Scrooge held his sister's gaze as tight as her
hand, trembling as he felt the truth of her words, but
couldn't speak. "I... I... don't know if I can." Young
Scrooge sniffed and wiped his eyes.

"Promise me you will try."

He could only nod, though he was not sure he
would ever be able to honor that promise.

"And promise me you'll watch over Fred." Fan
opened her eyes all the way and pulled their clasped
hand to her chest. "You will be his only connection to
me." Tears welled up in Fan's eyes as she smiled before
coughing again.

"Fan. I promise, but only if you will please stop talking like this. The doctors say you will recover," he lied as he reached for a clean rag to wipe his sister's brow. Her sweating had intensified with the coughing, and he could not keep the worry from showing on his face.

"Do not worry so much, Ebby. You will be a perfect role model and will do the family proud." She relaxed and settled back on her pillow. "Now, I need my rest. Please tell my husband not to disturb me for a few hours."

"I love you, Fan." Young Scrooge kissed the back of her hand before tucking her in gently. She didn't respond, either already dropped off to rest or perhaps the sickness had her now that she confirmed her son would be watched over.

The spirit bowed its head and closed its eyes as the room darkened slowly. Scrooge kept his eyes on Fan till the last blink of light.

"She died shortly after I left. For all I know I was the last person to talk to her." Scrooge sniffed, wiping his nose on his sleeve.

The very next day, Bentley sent Fred to live with a sister of his north of London, claiming a woman's care was what Fred needed. It wasn't for many years, not until after Bentley had passed away – not of consumption but of over-consuming – that Fred, now a young man ready to create his own way in the world, reached out to Scrooge to rekindle their relationship.

Scrooge wanted to be closer to Fred, but convinced himself that by keeping his nephew out of his life, he was caring for his nephew as his sister had asked.

If he and Marley were ever discovered, witnesses would be called. He worried Fred could be found guilty of protecting them and be punished, or at least socially outcast. Scrooge had extracted himself from his nephew's life out of fear for Fred's safety, but Fred continued to come back.

Now, Scrooge heard his sister's request for what it was, and not as he had convinced himself it had to be. He hadn't done as she asked. Oh, how the passage of time had crystallized the truth. He now saw his actions for what they were: empty excuses derived from fear rather than a true honoring of Fan's deathbed wishes.

Scrooge heaved a heavy sigh as he and the Ghost of Christmas Past floated through a thick fog and settled down on the front walk of an estate he would never forget. The realization stopped his breath. Scrooge battled warring emotions, feeling the twin weights of his sisters' death and his failure to honor her wishes alongside unabashed joy at seeing this place again. He had come here only once, the year after his sister's death. And what a Christmas it had turned out to be.

The Spirit raised its hand creating a light that beat back the haze and closeness of the mist. "You know this place?"

Scrooge swallowed again and licked his lips. "I could never forget it." Scrooge had exerted as much energy suppressing fond memories, such as this one, as he had the bad, but his heart wanted to remember.

Scrooge walked away from the safe glow of the spirit, hoping to get in the building, before the spirit could whisk him away once again. "Come on, they'll all be inside," he chided, only a little wary of the potential consequences of taking such a commanding tone with the ghost that controlled his memories and the physical manifestation of them.

Scrooge reached for the large manor door, but hesitated, knowing who he would see inside. The spirit encouraged him with a gentle hand forward. Scrooge sighed and then, grabbing for the handle, stumbled forward through the door and into the main foyer of the Fezziwig Estate.

The room was awash in the sounds of joviality and celebration and Scrooge was overcome with the smells of clove and roasted meat. A hundred candles cast their light to nuisance the fog and keep its dreariness outside. And everywhere, people. There were many he hadn't thought of in years, others he saw every day but usually didn't care to see. And a few others, still, more important to him than he would let himself acknowledge.

"Happy Christmas!" Mr. Fezziwig hollered from the room to his left. His excitement was met with similar calls of glad tidings, everyone pitching a cup or glass into the air and hugging arm and hand.

Scrooge was overcome with memories. "There's Dick Wilkins. He was pretty fond of me. I worked with him at Fezziwig's. And there's that Charles Darcy. This is the night I first met him."

"And her?" the spirit pointed to a beautiful woman standing next to the fire. A robin blue dress with white lace seams and hems, her cheeks rosy and her expression one of joy.

Scrooge let out the breath he had been holding, "Isabelle."

"Jacob Marley's sister." The spirit floated at Scrooge's shoulder. "You knew her well, too."

Scrooge shook his head. "There was a time I would say I knew her better than Jacob." He looked down and away from her smiling repose. "I pray she got what she wanted."

"And him? Did he get what he wanted?" The spirit pointed past Isabelle to a man leading the room in a song, a tune commonly sung wishing all well and happiness on this day and into the new year.

Scrooge only nodded. Isabelle took the signing man's hand and sang along, toasting him and smiling even more. Jacob Marley looked as light as a feather among the many partygoers, as he strained his voice to be heard above everyone as he carried them all into another chorus. How Marley was able to inspire everyone to feel so alive had always been a mystery, but one Scrooge had been drawn to immediately. He smiled and wiped his face again with his sleeve, this time without hiding or offering up excuses, as the song ended applause erupted around them.

Scrooge clapped along in spite of himself, until he caught the sight of his younger self, standing away from the crowd. Younger Scrooge held a full cup of grog and looked pensive, as if he wished he were anywhere else but there. Dick Wilkins waltzed by with one of Fezziwig's daughters and appeared, by contrast, to be truly enjoying himself. In the next moment, the happy couple stole a kiss under the mistletoe. Both Scrooges watched from the corner of the room, but it was the younger of them that began to down the entire contents of his glass in one gulp, dropping his glass on the table with a satisfactory exhale.

Young Scrooge filled another cup from the festive punch bowl, draining that as well in one gulp. He filled the cup a third time and raised it to his lips, stopping as he noticed Jacob Marley across the table from him, mouth agape.

"You must be thirsty." A wry smile played on Marley's features.

Young Scrooge downed the third glass. "It's good."

"It is. But I promise you, one more like that and you won't be upright much longer and there is still much yet to enjoy." He smiled a sideways grin, his tousled hair and cutting jaw flickered in the candlelight of the table. "I'm Jacob. And you are?" Scrooge looked on and felt his heart swoon in real time, in the same way it had that night.

"Ebeneezer Scrooge," responded with a slouch of his shoulders, unsure of what were Marley's intentions.

"Eb! You work for ol' Fezziwig. He told me all about you!" He smiled. "Why're you looking to ruin your night with too much grog?"

"I didn't want to come. Dick Wilkins said we would have a good time, and it might help me forget about... Well, forget about..." young Scrooge couldn't quite finish his thought.

"A bad Christmas perhaps?" Marley offered him a glass of water, his expression understanding.

Young Scrooge took the glass and nodded, offering no further explanation. "Just last year."

"Well then," Marley gripped Scrooge's shoulder, letting his hand linger a little longer than felt customary. "Eb. We must see what we can do to create better memories for you on this day and maybe help soften the pain that comes with its recollection." He put an arm around him and directed him back into the salon where a game of Blindman's Bluff was causing a raucous stir. Edith, the housemaid, had been cornered by one of the grooms, Joseph. She was flushed and shaking to hold back her laughter, but failing spectacularly as the groom continued to close in to catch her. Her tittering of laughter only egged him on.

Social norms dictated the servants should have their own celebration in their part of the estate, on a different day. But for Fezziwig, everyone celebrated together. Scrooge didn't think his former employer ever cared what people thought about it, but rather he seemed more concerned about making sure everyone was included and had a good time. To Fezziwig, Edith and Joseph were employees just like Scrooge. As Scrooge watched on, he remembered that it was one of the many things he had admired in the man. He struggled to embody the same courage in his own business, and now scolded himself silently for the way he had treated Cratchit.

Scrooge followed his younger self into the salon, remembering exactly what it was like to be tucked next to Marley's firm torso. Marley gestured to the soiree, still gripping tight and close to Scrooge. "We must join the game and get you out of your bad humor."

"But I don't know how to play."

"It's easy." Marley reached over and plucked the blindfold off the groom's head, now red faced with embarrassment at the sounds Edith had made. "Eb's next." Marley turned young Scrooge around and fixed the blindfold to his eyes. "Now, we disorient you. After I let go, you must search for someone in the room. Anyone. Whomever you find, you guess who it is."

Edith let out another peal of laughter. "And you have to kiss 'em if you're right." A scandalous, light-hearted gasp ran through the crowd. Joseph turned bright red again. He knew the rules but was too embarrassed to kiss Edith.

The spirit laughed at this. "You seemed eager to play the game. Especially the kiss part." The winking light of the spirit prodded a good-natured smile from Scrooge. He would have responded but was overcome by the moment. He knew what happened, he could never forget it. But now he would get to actually see how it had come to pass, as the time before he had experienced it from behind the blindfold.

Marley spun him three times, counting loudly with the rest of the room joining in. Young Scrooge stopped and almost toppled over, the effects of the Christmas cheer he chugged starting to have an effect. The crowd chuckled, trying to maintain secrecy of their location. Young Scrooge forced a half-hearted smile as he put his hands out in front of him to avoid running into any furniture.

Scrooge knew that his younger self was listening for the sounds of people moving around. He watched as everyone had stepped back at Marley's urging, including an indignant Belle, who folded her arms a look of concern creeping across her face as she scanned the crowd.

He watched as Marley pivoted and mirrored in reverse Scrooge's steps forward, dancing slow across the room, toward the fire. Until, Marley could back up no further. Giddied cries welled up around him, led most enthusiastically by Edith, as Scrooge laid a hand on Marley's chest.

"Ah Ha!" Young Scrooge exclaimed. "And now I decide who this is?"

"Yes," answered Marley but in a voice two pitches higher than his normal. More stifled laughter filtered from around him.

Young Scrooge knew it was Marley the moment he touched him. His pulse quickened and his mouth went dry. Scrooge watched as his younger self allowed his hand to linger across the man's chest and up his neck to the nose, causing laughter to break out again across the room. He mussed his hair as Marley protested and brought his own hands up, catching young Scrooge's in them. The two men were but half a step apart, now holding hands. "It's Jacob Marley, I believe." Scrooge grinned as the room erupted into applause and laughter again. Edith, feeling especially coquettish on Christmas, cried, "Now, you kiss 'em." before giggling to hysterics.

The room quieted as Marley removed Scrooge's blindfold. The two men looked eye to eye. Something twinkled in Marley's, a play at a joke or maybe some other mischief as he closed his eyes, exaggerating his puckering lips. At this, the crowd really wet their eyes with hysterics, several scarcely able to breathe. It was not customary for those of the same sex to partake in the kiss.

"Oh brother, you are a lark." Belle's quick smile did not quite reach her eyes. She downed her drink and left the room to the dining area.

Scrooge watched on with such anticipation; the moment forever burned into his soul. Oh, how he would have kissed him with such vigor if only the room had been empty and if only it had not been Christmas only a year after his dear sister's death and so many other if onlys. Perhaps even if he had known himself better, if he had been able to shed others' opinions and expectations, maybe, just maybe, he would have placed his lips on the man's and experienced for the first time what it could have been to connect to another human.

However, as it happened before, Mr. Fezziwig entered the room with another holler of his jovial voice, "Marley. Scrooge. Finally, you meet."

Marley scoffed, opening his eyes and stepping away from his new friend. "Fezziwig, you old prude, you interrupted my gift. I should think it is you who now owes me a kiss."

More vibrations of lighthearted laughter flowed through the room as young Scrooge smiled and stepped back. He covered his mouth self-consciously and felt his heart still hammering away in his chest. "Yes, sir. I hadn't known you were trying to get us to meet. If I had, I would have acted more professionally."

"Ah come, Ebeneezer," Fezziwig encouraged, pulling the young man under arm, and deftly moving to place Marley under the other. "It's Christmas, not a business gathering."

Scrooge watched as Fezziwig led the two men out of the room. "That's when he introduced us properly," Scrooge explained to the spirit. "Jacob was already working at the Exchange. He showed me around." Scrooge stalked his younger self through the room as he was guided by his rotund employer, remembering how truly happy he was in that moment.

The spirit pressed further, knowing Scrooge needed to remember these events. "And what of Fezziwig, what was he like?"

"An amazing man," Scrooge recollected with happiness, allowing some of the forgotten moments of the years lost in between to float up in his memory, seeing Mr. Fezziwig clearly.

"A great role model?" The spirit flashed a bright light. "One anyone would be blessed to work for."

Scrooge nodded. "Aye. He saw potential in me and never tried to stand in the way of my success, worried it might eclipse his own. I owe him more gratitude than I ever showed him." Scrooge swallowed hard, as the jovial sounds of celebration around him dimmed and grew fuzzy. Scrooge was once again confronted with his own behavior towards Bob Cratchit. He considered what it would be to treat him more in the way his old boss, Fezziwig, treated all of his employees.

"There is another Christmas with Jacob Marley." The spirit stretched its light forward, beckoning Scrooge to look. "Be strong. You must see the things you have chosen to forget."

Scrooge hung his head, wrapping his arms around his body, although there was no draft or cold north wind to chill the bone. He knew exactly where the spirit was taking him next, and thus was unable to look up. After a moment he heard the crackle of a wood fire and realized he had also closed his eyes.

"Our time together allows this last moment. You must open your eyes." The spirit urged.

Scrooge did as he was told, and was greeted by the floor, he recognized the bedchamber rug, but the room was much brighter than he had ever kept it, and it was not even daylight outside.

Steeling himself against more rising emotion, he looked up to see a version of himself, seven years younger to the day, sitting half saddle on the bed. Marley was tucked in, his eyes closed, face gaunt. Long lost was the face of the jovial party leader. The shrewd businessman. The charismatic statesman. Scrooge's soul pair.

"Oh," exhaled Scrooge. "Haven't I been haunted by this Christmas enough?" Scrooge moved closer to his younger self on the bed. He inched closer still, to get a better look at Marley. "He's still as handsome as ever, even like this."

Marley stirred and, upon opening his eyes, smiled. "Happy Christmas, Eb."

Marley lapsed into a coughing fit. Younger Scrooge poured a glass of water and offered it to him after the coughing ceased. "I fear I am sicker than we may have realized," Marley chuckled.

Scrooge watched his younger self gingerly wipe Marley's forehead with a damp cloth. "Don't say that." Young Scrooge wiped his eyes as he kissed the man. "After our first year together, you promised me at least forty Christmases together. Remember?"

Marley nodded his head, a slow rocking motion. "Eb, what we have is special, but it's come at a cost." Marley swallowed before starting to cough again.

Scrooge knew it was not the same illness that took his sister, but each raspy cough, reverberated loose the anchored memory of holding his sister's hand in much the same way. "You are not sick today because of our love, Jacob. I won't believe it."

Marley cleared his throat and closed his eyes again. "I know, Eb. My love for you has only made the world better for me." Marley shook their clasped hands. "But, if only just once I could have held your hand along the promenade in the park. The way we watched others do."

Scrooge's look softened, and he squeezed their clasped hands. "I hold your hand now."

"Or, I would have kissed you more." Marley grinned. "Remember our first?"

Both Scrooges nodded in unison. "At your parent's manor. On the first New Year's Day after we met at Fezziwig's."

"You were so scared," Marley chuckled.

The memories broke open as Scrooge watched their exchange. Their first kiss, the exhilaration of the clandestine encounter bolting the moment forever to his heart and soul.

Scrooge watched his younger self recharge the cool cloth to Marley's head, comforting him. "It could have been disastrous for us if anyone found out."

Marley swallowed, keeping his eyes closed. "We could have done it. We still could."

Young Scrooge kissed Marley on the forehead, "We will. I vowed to you an eternity of myself, and I intend to keep it," the younger Scrooge responded.

"I just hope you will be safer after I..." Marley coughed again.

"Don't say it." Scrooge laid his head on the recumbent Marley's bare chest. "I would do anything, if it meant keeping us together."

Both Scrooges wept.

"Don't cry my love." Marley's own tears rolling down, as he closed his eyes. "Remember the love we had for each other and try to share it with others." Marley managed to lay a tender hand to the side of the younger Scrooge's face as he relaxed and sank into a dreamless sleep.

Ebenezer Scrooge fell to his knees as the room started to fade. The light of the spirit withered and extinguished. "I love you, Jacob," he whispered in unison with the corporeal memory of his younger self as the room fell into darkness.

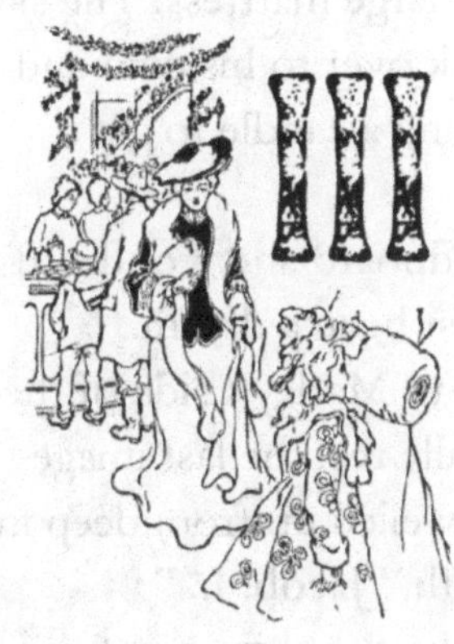

THE PRESENT

Scrooge struggled to release the memory of that night from seven Christmases ago, as he was slowly becoming aware of the nothingness around him. And yet, he felt grounded, seated even. The space was dark as a coal pitch; it smelled old and lonely. "What is this place you have brought me to now?" Scrooge noticed his voice didn't echo as he expected. "Spirit? Hello?"

Nothing.

Scrooge started to panic as something weighed him down. "Spirit! Help! Have I gone blind?!" He felt his throat tightening as he screamed for help and thrashed around violently; only to find he had been in his bed all along, trapped under his covers. He gulped for breath as relief washed over him. "I'm in my room," he assured himself.

He sniffled and wiped his nose with the back of his sleeve. His face was wet. "But, of course," he scolded himself. "Where else would I be at this time of night?"

Scrooge looked around. He *was* in his bed, but all the way on the other side of the large mattress. The side he never slept on. He rolled back over to his own and checked the bedside clock, lighting a candle to get a better look. Almost midnight.

He sat back against the headboard and wondered how it was possible, had it all just been a dream. However, when he looked back to Marley's side of the bed, he recalled just how viscerally real the last images he had seen. Tears and sadness welled up from deep in his soul. He inhaled a deep breath. "Jacob. I..."

His confession interrupted by the chiming of the hour. With it, a bright light issued from the sitting room. It was so bright, even from behind Scrooge's closed bedroom door, he found himself very grateful for the barrier between them.

"Come here, Scrooge, or I'll come get you." A booming voice rattled the curtain rings and shook the door.

Scrooge pulled himself out of bed. He didn't want to find out the hard way if the new spirit was capable of following through on his threat. "I'm coming," he managed as he stepped into his slippers and to the door.

When Scrooge opened it, he was nearly blinded, this spirit's light many times brighter than that of the previous one. Never had Scrooge imagined that the light of the deceased would burn so intensely. Scrooge shielded his eyes as he tried to look around the room.

"Too bright for you?"

Scrooge nodded. The light receded, and what a change to his sitting room did he behold. The room had been transformed into a celebration Ol' Fezziwig would've approved of. The room was filled to the brim with delicious looking treats and gifts wrapped with brown packaging paper, painted in every festive color. There appeared a table with several large bowls of piping hot mashed root vegetables sitting around a large roasted duck, and behind that, a roasted turkey. There was a goose on a spit over his fireplace, attended by a green-robed, giant of a man. He sported a beard full enough to match his booming voice as he bid Scrooge come nearer.

The giant's jovial smile and the festive bounty surrounding him lowered Scrooge's guard a bit. Scrooge approached and more fully took in the room. Every wall was covered in holly and pine boughs. Garlands of paper snowflakes traversed the room. Candles of many colors burned bright, casting a soft, warm glow about the room. Never had it been so festively dressed. "And who might you be?" Scrooge asked, mustering more confidence than he'd managed in the presence of the previous spirit.

The giant figure laughed as he basted the goose before turning his attention to the aging money lender. "That should be obvious. Have you not seen anyone like me before?"

"Never." Scrooge cleared his throat.

"You look to be a man that should have seen at least sixty-five of my siblings?"

Scrooge regarded the ghost with astonishment. "So many! But I would remember one such as yourself. Are you all similarly built?"

"I assure you that, while we each would claim to be different, there are similarities enough that you would be able to place any one of us." The ghost put hands on his hips, his solid hairy chest and abdomen puffed forward through the break in the green robe. His rosy cheeks framed his smile. "I am the Ghost of Christmas Present. Look around and see the cornucopia of potential this day represents." Scrooge took in the abundance and felt a merry sense overcome him, a burgeoning desire to allow himself to experience even a little of the pleasure being offered.

"Who'll eat all this? I scarcely could in a year's time. And what's all this mess?" Scrooge pointed at the decorations. "Mrs. Dilber isn't going to like having to clean all of that up. Not at all."

The bearded ghost laughed, a deep bellowing sound, his chest shaking. He wrapped the robe tighter to him, as it threatened to slip its way off. "Scrooge. They warned me of your taciturn and reluctant nature, but no one apprised me of your sense of humor." The ghost surely mocked him, but something in the twinkling of his gentle eyes freed Scrooge to laugh a little as well.

"No. I suppose no one would think that," Scrooge harrumphed, recalling that at one time he was rather clever with words and could make Marley laugh out loud. "Well, not anymore."

The giant ghost drew closer to the man. "After this night, I pray you would imagine yourself so. Perhaps recalling a self that still exists, buried beneath all the excuses, all the sadness, all the greed you shelter in."

"What is it you would show me? If it is my Christmas present you are to show me, I can save you the trouble. It will likely be me sitting in my office all day, beside the dwindling fire, avoiding any knock at my door from giddy carol singers."

The giant chuckled again. "I am sure you tell the truth. Take my hand." The giant ghost approached him, extending his arm. "Instead, let us see how those around you make merry on this festive day."

Reluctant, but less so than with the last spirit, Scrooge placed his hand in the giant's, noting how it almost disappeared in the grasp. The room popped into a wash of glimmering brightness. Color and light swirled around him before eventually settling back into a configuration that wasn't his room but rather, a different one. This sitting room was a warm and comfortable space with plenty of seating, treats and decorations for the holiday. Most of the chairs were occupied by at least a dozen adults and there were several children crawling around, demanding something from each other in their play.

Scrooge gasped as his nephew Fred entered with a tray full of close-to-overflowing glasses of wine. Just behind him entered a fetching woman who Scrooge had never met, but was likely his niece-in-law, Clara.

"Do you know where we are?" The ghost's presence loomed over Scrooge. It appeared to be able to exist around people without bothering them. In fact, as it moved about the room, and drew near to a person, they seemed to glow and brighten, as if lit from within.

Scrooge nodded but watched the people in the room inquisitively. "Are you doing that to them? Making them happy?"

The ghost halted; a sincere expression softened the wrinkles around the jovial ghost's eyes. "I exude the essence of generosity and understanding. It is the gift of Christmas I provide and those around who are in need or want of it can feel my presence."

Scrooge wondered if he might also have been brought under the ghost's spell and was about to ask, when his nephew began clinking a glass with the handle of a spoon, quieting the room. "Ladies and gentlemen." Everyone settled into a spot and focused their attention on their genial host. "It's that time every year I ask you all to raise a glass and send a well wish to one of my most esteemed and well-regarded kin, Ebeneezer Scrooge."

Scrooge looked at the robed ghost, incredulous that not only did his nephew toast him well, but that, apparently, he set aside a time every year to do so. Scrooge was awash in the guilt.

The gathering of revelers yawned and groaned, some good-naturedly, while others drew in their faces as if they had tasted lemon instead of grape. "Not that again," said a man standing behind Scrooge. Scrooge knew that voice and turned to see Charles Darcy smiling, face red, drink in hand. "Fred, I have come to your house every year for as long as I can remember and not only have I *never* seen your uncle here, but I also know him to be a wretched and parsimonious type." The gentleman chortled.

"I thought Charles liked me?" Scrooge narrowed his gaze at the man.

The ghost dismissed him. "Oh, he does. See how he smiles."

"Never were you wrong Charles," Fred explained. "Truly, Scrooge is one of the most vile and miserable old codgers you could ever hope to avoid running across in your very worst of days. Worse than imagination."

The party guests all nodded in agreement and the ghost bellowed another laugh next to Scrooge, throwing his head back.

"Finding this funny?" Scrooge scowled.

"Just listen. You'll see." The ghost never stopped smiling.

Nephew Fred continued, "You see, Charles, I do wish him well and I hope someday he comes to his senses and realizes all the lovely things in this world he is missing that wouldn't actually cost him a penny if he would just let a little happiness in." Fred looked around the room at all his guest, glass raised. "And as long as I can wish him well and truly mean it, then I know I have found the spirit of Christmas and my mother would be proud."

Everyone nodded again and agreed with a rousing, "To Scrooge!"

Fred added, "Were he here, we would wish long life to him and to us all."

Niece Clara raised her glass. "Were he here, we'd all be witness to a Christmas miracle." She winked at her husband and took a drink.

Scrooge knew he owed them an apology for all the years he was absent from the family meals and holidays; she genuinely seemed to want to get to know him. The realization made him feel sad all over again.

Clara cleared her throat. "All right, all right, you all. No more speeches. Move all these chairs out of the way. We will have singing and dance. And Blindman's Bluff!" Everyone cheered her on as she began clearing trays of food, making a space in the center of the room. "What first?" she asked no one in particular, but everyone answered.

"Games!"

Scrooge watched as the handkerchief found its way first to a woman that, he guessed, was one of Clara's sisters. She favored Clara in appearance but exuded a more youthful, giddy energy. She spun around three times as the guests all moved away, trying not to laugh and jostle one another.

The sister giggled incessantly as she moved around, gesticulating her arms in front of her, as though she were looking for someone in particular. Her cheeks were rosy with merriment. Scrooge couldn't stop the ache that sprung up where his heart was purported to be, as he remembered the time Marley had first shown him how to play the game.

"I would have kissed him." Scrooge said, shaking his head. He looked up at the party goers noting the sister had finally caught her target. "Kiss. Kiss. Kiss. Kiss." He joined in the chanting as it grew in volume and intensity. He felt suddenly swept up by the merriment of the moment, and all at once, felt years younger.

His smile dimmed as he noticed the tingling of happiness just at the periphery of his skin; recognizing the aura of the ghost coming closer.

"We must move on," came its voice now more determined than jovial.

"But, I want to see if they kiss." Scrooge pulled back, but it was too late. The room was brightening into a now familiar, glimmering explosion. This time, they reassembled onto a street corner in a poorer area of town. Scrooge sighed, defeated. "But I wanted to see."

"Then you should go to Christmas lunch at your nephew's." The ghost gave his charge a reproachful look. "Start living your life again. See what wonder you can find."

Scrooge nodded, beginning to understand what he might have been missing all those years. But then he frowned when he took stock of his surroundings. "Why have you brought me to this forsaken area of town?"

"It's possible to be festive here as well. In fact, you will see it is, perhaps, even more possible than in other places where there is more money and bounty at hand. Here, you will see what you have provided." He pointed to the small door of a tiny cottage nestled among many other similar two-story versions. "This is the estate of one Robert Cratchit. View the splendor of the holiday his salary provides."

Scrooge stepped up to the dirty multi-paned window of his bookkeeper and his family. The sound of children singing seeped out into the street. "I know this tune." Scrooge wiped his nose with his sleeve before putting it to the windowpane to cleanse it. "I used to sing it as a lad."

"And on Christmas day. We will know the way. To sing such sounds of happiness. God Bless us everyone."

Scrooge was vaguely aware the song had more words, but the children continued to repeat these same four lines. Scrooge smiled at the Cratchit family, unsure if it was the song, or the feelings of joy and togetherness they exuded, that moved him. Scrooge observed that while the children were all singing, one voice in particular rose above the rest.

"Enjoying yourself?" The ghost chuckled.

Scrooge folded his arms feeling scolded, but he still had a sense of cheer about him. "It's hard not to enjoy a song when it's sung with such beautiful voices. I hadn't known Bob's kids to be so talented. And so many children," Scrooge remarked with surprise. "I thought he only had a son and a daughter."

The Ghost of Christmas Present let out a mocking gasp. "Really? You had taken even that little interest in the life of your only employee." He looked down on Scrooge. "As you can see, there are five children. How could it be that you forgot about the twins and the youngest, Tim."

Scrooge looked back through the window. He knew the two eldest. He nodded to himself. "I stopped paying attention after...well, after the oldest two, it would seem."

"You stopped paying attention long before that, even. You were never good at the personal lives of others," the ghost poked.

Scrooge smiled in spite of the criticism. "True. It was Jacob who always reminded me of birthdays and other occasions. I guess after he passed, I didn't have..."

"To Mister Scrooge, we raise a glass." Scrooge looked utterly stricken with disbelief as he bent to regard the Cratchit family closer through the window. Another one raising a glass in his honor? Surely, this was a joke, it would be what Scrooge deserved.

Bob was raising aloft a water glass filled with a dark liquid. He wore a proud face with rosy cheeks, surrounded by six other faces, sporting disapproving frowns.

Mrs. Cratchit, or so Scrooge presumed since he hadn't ever met her, was the first to speak. "Coo! Why do you do this to us? Here we are meant to be merry, and you go and say that name."

Bob gazed at his wife with loving eyes. "Emily? My dear. I know your feelings, but you don't see him as I do." Bob lowered his glass slightly, enough to look each member of his family in the eyes. "He is so sad and alone now."

"'Tis own fault for that, innit," she responded. "And the way he treats you my dear."

Scrooge watched as the children's heads moved back and forth between their parents. Timidly, the youngest cleared his throat. "Maybe it takes a beautiful day like today to find a way to wish happiness to those that wouldn't do the same for us."

Emily Cratchit looked at her youngest son and then at her spouse, lost for words. "Of course it is, Tim." A wry smile graced her lips as she put a hand to her hip. "Now, how is it my youngest is the wisest?"

Tim lowered his gaze but held his glass aloft. "Because I would try to be strong like father and bless the boys at my school who aren't kind to me."

A single tear made its way down the young boy's face, and his twin siblings, one on each side, threw an arm around him.

Speaking together, the twins explained that though they had done what they could, Tim was constantly pestered by three older boys, usually on the way home from school. This was often the reason why Tim was late getting home; he had to take a different way home.

Scrooge felt an anger rising in him, reminded of times he was bothered by boys older than he, for being different.

Bob and Emily shared a glance and reached for one another. Emily broke the silence. "Children, we will speak of this more tomorrow. But, for tonight, we will enjoy ourselves and each other in the safety of this home your father provides for us." Bob squeezed her hand tighter; she looked up at him. "Oh, and since it is Christmas I'll even toast ta that old so-and-so Scrooge. May he live long and bless 'im."

"God bless us, everyone," Tim sang as he raised his glass, his eyes red but a smile on his face as he drank with the rest of his family.

Bob then set about giving out gifts. The girls opened clothes their mother had made for them; new shawls and scarfs, warm things crafted with love that would offer protection on cold days. The elder boy opened a set of cricket bats. "Thank you, father." The young man regarded the gift, swinging and parrying as if he were a professional. His eager enthusiasm caused his younger sisters to giggle. "Careful, Peter," his mother half-heartedly warned.

Scrooge was particularly interested in what gift Tim would get from his family. He watched as the young boy opened what looked like a feather pen and ink. Tim hugged his father and mother with abandon as he chattered on about all the songs and stories he could write now that he had a pen.

The Ghost of Christmas Present made a show of clearing his throat. "I imagine you will now go count all your pens and ink jars at your office. But you will find none missing. Bob purchased this on his own, working at the exchange in addition to the many hours you already demand."

Scrooge shook his head. "Impossible. One of my colleagues would've told me if he were working for them," he scoffed.

"Not for the exchange, though he is smart enough to apprentice with any of your rivals. But at the exchange, changing oil lamps and bringing in coal to keep the fires going." Scrooge's heart dropped. He hadn't ever considered Cratchit would have to work elsewhere in order to support his family.

"Oh, Spirit." Scrooge shook his head. "I didn't know."

"Nor would he want you to. You aren't the only one that's too proud to say when you need help."

Scrooge peered back in at the family. "Such a small meal. And yet, so much love." He felt his voice crack, but it was obviously a measure of the cold night air and nothing else. "I pay him so little." His voice dropped away as the family dissolved into a pop of glimmering colors; shards of silver, gold, reds, and greens danced around the time travelers.

"This will be our last stop, Scrooge." The room materialized around them as the ghost's voice returned to him. At first the space felt familiar, but not in the way his old school yard had, rather in the way a joyful memory would affect you the first time you remembered it. "Do you know this place?"

Scrooge squinted as he looked around. He took in a hearth with a roaring fire, and chairs for four and a settee circled a low table covered with gifts. There were candles lit atop many surfaces, shelves of books, and glass cases of evergreen and red flowers. Scrooge and the ghost stood on a rug of dark fiber. He was just about to mention how familiar it all felt when a woman entered. She was his age and the smile lines that marked her face belied the joyful life she'd lived. "Belle." His voice caught in his throat.

"Ah, you do know this place," the ghost pressed him.

"It's Jacob's family home. It should be his. It was supposed to be, but he chose me..."

Belle cleared her throat. "Everyone, in here! Look what your grandpapa has done for you." A troop of children, adults, and some in between, all talking and laughing at once, entered the room, settling into every available seat and cranny in order to be as close as possible to the pile of gifts at the center of the room.

A man Scrooge recognized as his former colleague, Dick Wilkins, entered the room and put an arm around Belle's waist. Only then did he recall that they married a few years after that Christmas when Marley had shown Scrooge how to play Blindman's Bluff.

"She looks to be well." Scrooge said with a hint of remorse. He had known her well when he and Marley were first in business together.

"You will see. It is Christmas, but not everyone is happy. It is a normal human emotion, sadness. It knows all seasons but can be particularly isolating when everyone around is feeling joy." He gestured to Belle, who held Wilkins' hand as the family dove into the pile of wonders. Scrooge watched as her eyes wandered the room and seemed to rest on him.

For a second, terror pinned him in place. "Can she see me?" But, then Scrooge thought to turn around. Directly behind him was an oil painting. A young Jacob Marley, above the mantel in a place of prominence. Scrooge gulped. "Oh, I forgot about that." His heart leapt at seeing the Marley's dashing silhouette, "She took it from our apartment after he died."

Belle nodded at her brother's image. Taking a drink with eyes brimming, she returned the squeeze of her husband's hand and entered the melee of her family's festivities.

"She looks so sad. But she never responded to any message I sent her. Not even when I wrote to tell her how sick Jacob was." Scrooge looked at the ghost for guidance.

"Those are past Christmases. My realm is of the present. However, I don't see any malice in her heart. Just anguish and regret." The ghost walked out of the room and towards the door but paused on the hall steps with a loud exhale. "The same I see in yours."

Scrooge reflected on the last time he was in this room. It was the last of numerous warm holiday and family gatherings to which Scrooge had been welcomed by the Marley's. But on this occasion, Jacob's father found out about their relationship.

Belle let the secret slip, she claimed, accidentally. Marley and his father had a terrible fight. And at the end, his father vowed that if Marley left with Scrooge, he would say he'd never had a son. Belle remained silent through it all, eyes cast down, avoiding looking at either of them, as Marley and Scrooge exited the home for the last time.

The next time he saw her was the day after Marley died. She couldn't even offer him a condolence. She strode into their apartment building, seizing whatever she could find from Marley's apartment. Thankfully, Scrooge had the foresight to move some things to the apartment across the hall before she reached the top floor. Scrooge hadn't been strong enough to go in after her; he was too heartbroken. Unfortunately, he forgot about Marley's portrait.

The clock in the hall chimed the hour. In response, the ghost began to glow and sparkle. "My time has come." The large, robed ghost levitated. "I must leave you now, Scrooge."

"But I have so much more I can learn from you." Scrooge dropped to his knees, pulling at the ghost's jovial holiday robe. "I assure you, I am not the man you first met. I have been changed."

"As happy as I am to hear that, it will require more than words to change for good. Fear not the future as mankind does. But go towards it with an open mind and heart full of love."

The ghost continued to rise as the clock chimed a final gong of midnight. Scrooge held his grip on the hem of the large robe, until it gave way, and he dropped to the floor covered by the sprawling garment. He felt around under the heavy cloak, his chest tightening. "I can't breathe."

He started to flail again, as he had after the first journey, before remembering himself. "I must be in my bed again." He took a deep, cleansing breath, and chuckled to himself as he found the edge and pulled the cover back.

But yet, he was not in his bed, rather still on the hallway floor of the Marley estate. He crept on hands and knees from under the heavy dark cloak, which was no longer a vibrant green. Confused, and a little afraid, he brought himself to stand.

 WHAT MIGHT BE

Scrooge looked around, wondering why he hadn't returned to his bed this time. Suddenly, the cloak began rolling around the floor. A dark shadow took a human-like shape, taller even than the jolly Ghost of Christmas Present. The phantom remained covered, not giving away an inch of what form lay underneath.

Scrooge waited for an announcement or an introduction for a short moment before growing impatient at the silence. "Am I in the presence of the Ghost of Christmas Future?"

The shadow fabric shape inclined its top forward, where the head would be, as in a way to nod yes, it was in fact as Scrooge had assumed. While its hearing was intact it couldn't speak. The future has no voice.

"I know your purpose is for my welfare and while I am terrified of what you will show me, I know it is to help." Scrooge wrung his hands, wiped them on the pockets of his gown, and nervously moistened his lips. "Lead on."

The shadow shape moved a little side-to-side. An appendage separated from the dark form and stuck out parallel to the floor. It seemed to be pointing back to the room Scrooge had just exited with the other ghost.

"In there?" Scrooge looked up at the shrouded figure as he slowly stepped away from it, back in the direction from which he'd just come. The phantom inclined its head forward in a single bow.

Scrooge peaked around the corner, uncertain what he would see. Clearly, a different day was manifest before him. Belle was standing, hands folded, staring up at her brother's painting above the fireplace. It was no longer nighttime, as daylight poured in through the windows behind her. With tears in her eyes, she sniffed and wiped her cheek with a handkerchief. She looked as though she had been crying for some time. Dick Wilkins entered and crossed the room with long steps. "Belle. I know it hurts you. I knew them, too. But we have to get rid of it."

Belle pulled at her husband's shoulder. "Put it in the attic. No one will look there."

"We are fortunate that many have forgotten you were related. Think of our children." Dick stepped towards the fireplace. "Our grandchildren."

Belle shoulders fell forward and returned the handkerchief to her face.

"It was only a matter of time before the truth came

out," she wept. "I should have done more to help protect them."

Scrooge was gripped with terror. "Does she mean…?" But he knew. The life he and Marley had worked meticulously to keep hidden had been revealed. Scrooge slumped forward, only to have his attention jerked back at the sound of Dick pulling the portrait of Marley from the wall. With a quick movement, he tossed it in the fire. Scrooge and Belle gasped in unison.

"We have to destroy it." Dick Wilkins didn't look malicious. In fact, he looked truly sorrowed. "I am deeply sorry, Isabelle. But it is the only way. It's more than sinful, it's criminal. If anyone ever knew that we knew…People get sent to prison for knowing and not saying something."

Belle's gaze was transfixed on the brighter white rectangular residual, where the frame previously lived on the wall. "I refuse to ever believe my brother did anything wrong."

Dick put an arm around her as he watched the paint bubble and melt into the fire, releasing dark smoke and an acrid smell into the room. Scrooge pushed around them and tried to reach in the fire and pull it out, his hands swiping through the flames, feeling no heat or burn.

"I never should have let father send him out. I knew what was going on. And I didn't care. I loved them both" She dabbed her cheek again. "Well, after I got over the fact that *I* was their chaperone and not the other way around." She laughed a small sound. "And, I wouldn't have met you if it weren't for Ebenezer."

She gently put a hand to Dick's chest. "I feel like I'm losing my brother and my friend all over again."

Scrooge felt the phantom looming over him. The shadow stretched and yawned into each corner of the room, extinguishing the light of the fire, leaving the room raven black.

He felt the pull of gravity, as if not he, but the world around him was moving, while he stood still. He wailed an unrecognizable sound of terror.

As suddenly as the movement began, it stopped and the world around him materialized into a rainy London Street, one he knew well. Scrooge looked up the short block steps to the doors of the Exchange. Around, many people shuffled past each other going on about their days, coats and shawls wrapped tight, puffs of breath vaporizing in the air, suggesting it was not only a dreary foggy rain, but also freezing cold.

Charles Darcy walked past them, deep in conversation with two other men Scrooge recognized.

"I don't know who else they interrogated to uncover the information, but it has been verified," Darcy whispered, blowing into his hand to warm them.

Another man scoffed and regarded his colleagues with a severe look. "Well, most of us suspected. But what was it to me? I didn't want him looking to get me in his debt." He scoffed and then sneered, "Bet the Crown takes the estate, being a felony and all."

The third man nodded, looking even more unsympathetic than the other two. "Quite right," he spat. "It's only what he deserves, anyway."

Darcy sighed. "Perhaps I would feel differently had he not been so horrific. I mean, it's not like anyone got hurt..."

"You seem awfully taken by him, Mister Darcy. One might wonder if perhaps there wasn't something between you." The larger man raised a brow at him.

Darcy bristled. "I am quite sure I don't know what you mean. It's not like I knew. I had nothing to add to the investigation, though they interrogated me too."

The spitter spat again and stepped closer, clearing his throat. "Enough of this. I care not what was done, or who knew what. There's a lot of money and opportunity wrapped up in this. Maybe it'd be best for all of us to talk with the exchequer first thing tomorrow. See how the loans and holdings are going to be divvied up. I wouldn't mind helping in the redistribution of the wealth, if there's anything left after Little Vic gets done with it."

Charles Darcy nodded and lagged behind a little as the other two men laughed. Then, the street went dark, and the nothingness of the phantom's cloak enveloped him again.

Scrooge felt helpless as the shadow took over the vision again. "All of that planning and careful consideration. Keeping everyone away from us, family, friends. And it still came out." Scrooge noted Darcy seemed to be the most unsettled of the three men. Marley and he had been friends long before Scrooge met them; it's likely Darcy had been a confidant all along, quietly keeping their secret.

The scene returned. It was the same rainy gray and fog, but at least he was inside a dwelling or shop of some kind.

Scrooge regarded a man of many more years than he, whistling a little tune as he dropped a meat of some kind into a bowl. The gesture encouraged several feral-looking cats of questionable cleanliness out from under a table toward the bowl. "There you go, my beauties."

The door burst open. A woman, carrying a full basket, hurricaned in and slammed the door shut with her backside. A moment of surprised silence passed between the two figures before they both dissolved into a cackling, triumphant laugh. It was Mrs. Dilber. She hiked up her hem and skipped around clicking her heels as if she were a little girl again. The large basket she carried seemed as light as a feather and she dropped it on the table between them.

"So, Missus Dilber, what have you found for us?" The man stood at the table, hands on his hips.

She cackled again. "They tried to keep me out, but I gots a key for the back dor, you see. Let me'self in. Wasn't none the wiser. Got a Bobby out front watchin' being as it's all goin' ta the Crown, I'd expect."

"Good. Good." He started to paw through the blankets and towels on top of the basket. "This looks like laundry."

She scoffed at him. "Had'ta make it look convincin' Joe. Besides this set never been slept in." She laughed as she pulled back the topmost layers and revealed something of wonder to the man. "See."

Joe leaned forward with large eyes. "Well. Good sakes Missus Dilber. What have we here?" He reached in and pulled out a small wooden box. The man spun it in his hands and stroked the top of it with a gentle hand before looking back in the basket for other items.

"Got all 'is good linens, and the brass from the cupboard. Hid most'a last time I cleaned." She looked proud of herself. "Bein' as I knew when they's comin' for 'im. Won't make *me* work 'nother Chrissmas day."

"Oooohhh," Joe said with wonder as he opened the wooden treasure. "Velvet lined. And what's this?"" He pulled out a silver chain with a pocket watch attached.

Scrooge knew it was truly something special, something he shouldn't have forgotten. A Christmas gift from Marley. "Jacob gave me that. The same year I gave him one." Scrooge smiled, recalling the look of surprise they shared when they exchanged similar boxes.

Scrooge watched as Joe tossed the box aside and attached the chain to his waist, placing the watch in his own pocket. Scrooge was overcome with a deep rage, and he swung out at the man, his fist moving easily through Joe's body. "That's mine."

Old Joe raised an eyebrow. "I'm surprised you even found something so nice. Wasn't anyone else there?"

"Nah. If on'y he'd been more natural like, someone'uld of been there ta care for'em after he pass'd." Mrs. Dilber nodded with a definitive motion and a scowl on her face.

Scrooge watched Old Joe fondle the watch, flipping it back and forth in the dim candlelight. His chest felt heavy, and his legs grew weak with guilt. Scrooge was certain he hadn't laid eyes on the watch in many years. Marley's had been buried with him.

"What's this?" Old Joe paused his flip-flopping motion of his hand and brought the item closer to the candlelight. "An inscription, Missus Dilber. We've come across not only a nice item, but a family heirloom."

"Ye ken charge double now." She rubbed her hands together greedily and Scrooge detested her now more in this moment than he did Old Joe.

"Let's see now. It says, *'to thine own self be true'*."

Mrs. Dilber scrunched her face, shaking her head. "Likely anyone could'a make their own meaning outta that anyway Joe. You'll get good blunt for'it."

The watch caught the light, reflecting and dancing it across the faces of Joe and Mrs. Dilber as the light of the candle extinguished and the subtle brightness from the small window faded to black. Scrooge felt a chilling discomfort as the phantom's essence and robe enveloped him. He focused his attention on a white window that was growing in size and brightness as it moved towards him.

He came face to face with the now familiar window of Bob Cratchit's. Scrooge was immediately overcome with relief. He shared with the phantom that in this future full of bleakness and nightmare there would be comfort in seeing a house full of joy and love.

Yet, as they approached, there was only silence emanating from the home. No sounds of excitement or merriment. No singing songs of Christmas.

"Why's it so quiet?"

The being lifted a side of its large form, which congealed into an arm, and pointed at the window.

Scrooge peered in, but he only saw a mother and son near the fireplace. She was holding a cloth to the young man's face and lines of worry deepened her brow, aging the handsome woman.

"Hones'ly, Tim. If you'd only just play the games with the other boys, this wouldn'ta happen. They only bother you so 'cause you don't do what they're doin'."

An older looking Tim than the last time Scrooge saw him, took the cloth from his mother, and wet it again with warm water off the hob. There was a red mark under his left eye, blood crusted under his nose, and a cut in his lip. He moved his left arm gingerly as well and appeared to be trying to splint it himself.

"I know, mother. It's just that I don't think it would matter." He put the cloth back to his face. "They don't like me. Because I'm different."

Mrs. Cratchit stiffened at the word "different" and stood taller. "You're my son. There's nothin' wrong with ya. Just boys being boys. You'll see. Someday they'll leave you alone." She bent back down and put his hand in hers. "Now, outside and wash up a bit. Dry your eyes. We wouldn't want to show weak eyes to your father when he gets home."

Tim nodded and stood, pushed his chair back so he could go and do as his mother had asked. Mrs. Cratchit followed her son with her eyes, blinking back tears as she lamented she could not protect him better.

Once he was safely out of earshot, she sat stiff as a board in her chair "Peter?" She called out to the empty room "You just watched it happen. As if I am to believe you didn't join in."

"I didn't, mother. Honest." Peter, the Cratchit's eldest, appeared from around the stairs to the upper level. "You don't know how it is. I try and stop them, but they don't listen and there's three of them. Once they came after me too, but I'm faster than Tim."

Mrs. Cratchit knew her son was being honest and recognized that if it weren't for his strong shoulders, he would likely have taken the same beating her youngest had. "I know, Peter," she sighed. "If only he would try to fit in."

Scrooge stepped back from the window, the echo of his own father yelling at him to act like a boy and behave like a boy should, reverberating around him.

"It's not enough to help Cratchit, is it? I need to help them all. Is that why you would show me this moment." He peeked back through the window trying to glimpse Tim's return. But felt he had intruded enough. He nodded to himself, resolute in his desire to help the whole Cratchit family, somehow.

Scrooge turned to look at the phantom feeling a sense of courage from his new purpose. "What is to come of me? I know my stuff was stolen and no one wants to be associated with me or Jacob. Am I dead?"

The phantom answered by engulfing him in his large black robes as he once again felt the world around him move while he stood still. Scrooge wasn't sure what he hoped he would see next, but his gut told him they were traveling even further into the future.

They arrived at a gated door in a dark and musty hallway. In front of him stood a man dressed in an officer's uniform, idly spinning a ring of keys. "And don't think I'm not generous, this being the day of the birth of our Lord. Not that any of you lot ever can expect to meet'em, but those'a ya work hard enough get an extra spoon of slop for dinner."

Another guard chuckled as he walked into the room, slapping his wooden club in the palm of this other hand. "Happy Christmas. Now get goin'."

Scrooge followed the phantom into the room. He observed a row of men all facing away from him, standing on wooden planks. They were clad in threadbare gray-blue jackets that hung off of them like spectral images themselves. In unison, they stepped forward lurching the gears of the machine that crushed rocks under the movement of their dispirited march. The sounds of the cracking and pulverizing rocks were more and more deafening with each step the miserable and dejected men took.

"Hard labor?" Scrooge muttered. "Oh! Please, no." He looked up and down the row of men. One had started to slow. The guard was immediately at his back, pressing the edge of the club into his backside, laughing. "No? I thought you liked that kinda thing." Several of the other men next to him shuddered and quickened their steps.

Scrooge moved closer to the poor soul who had been ridiculed by the guard. He needed only a moment to recognize an elderly version of himself.

His heartbeat quickened, and eyes widen with fear, as he watched himself slow down again. The guard came over, raising his club. "No." Scrooge stood in front of himself, but the club came down through him and connected with the elderly man. He turned his head and was spared having to see the injuries, but the sounds of flesh squashing and bones crunching, as the club came down at least three more times, made him ill.

His eyes wet with tears as he cupped his face in his hands. "How long have I been here?" He looked at the phantom as the black of the robe started to grow. "You wouldn't show me this unless there was a chance, a possibility, I could avoid this horror…right?" Scrooge implored the phantom.

Scrooge felt his body lifting toward the ceiling. The darkness of the room deepened. The phantom came closer. A face appeared through the hood, mouth bandaged shut, menacing eyes. Scrooge gasped in horror at the face of the phantom. As he tried to run, he found he was standing on the rock crushing machine.

He screamed as the machine moved underneath him. He was cuffed in manacles with chain links the size of wagon wheels, much larger than what Marley had worn during his earlier visit. He pulled fruitlessly at the chains as he felt the club prodding and striking him. He gasped and cried out, "No! Please! I am changed. Believe me! I will show them, Jacob, I will show everyone."

The machine cared not for Scrooge's plea and instead sped faster. Scrooge couldn't keep up. The many chain links grew heavier and more cumbersome. He shrieked a final sound as his legs dropped and he was dragged under the machine into the pulverized rock below.

A SECOND CHANCE

His whole body ached but no longer felt heavy. He opened his eyes slowly and looked down at his arms and legs, seeing he was back in his dressing gown. He sat up. "I'm in my room."

Yes, the bed was his, the curtains were his, the room was his. Everything was as it had been. Everything except for Scrooge, who was totally and completely changed. As Scrooge recalled the horrors and joys he had experienced at the grace of the ghosts, he vowed to amend his life into one full of gratitude and affection for mankind. He would undoubtedly remember the lessons of the spirits and that of Christmas itself. But most especially, he would remember his love for Jacob Marley.

"Oh, Jacob." He slumped out of the bed and onto his knees. "I will honor your life, Jacob, and I will love mine with a heart full of gratitude." Scrooge hung his head and cried. He didn't know if he could possibly right all his past wrongs, nor did he anticipate that anyone would believe him a changed man. But he had to try. He had to save Marley from an eternity of pain. "And I will devote my life, or what I have left, to making our past faults just."

Collecting himself from the floor, Scrooge crossed to his bureau and opening the top drawer for the first time in seven years, found the wooden box with the velvet lining. He pulled out the pocket watch, kissed the inscription on the back. The watch had lost its time, but that could be fixed.

"Gracious! Forget the time. I haven't any idea what day it is, but, whatever the day, it must only be dawn." Scrooge put the watch in his dressing gown pocket and ran to his window and saw that a gentle snow had been falling. He pushed the pane forward and, looking to the street below, saw a small child carting a sled.

"Young lad!" Scrooge hollered down. "A good day to you."

The boy looked confused as he recognized the man by the apartments he shouted from. He responded with caution, certain he had done something to upset the old, nasty man, even though, there was something different in his voice, a hint of joy even. "Good day, sir." He stopped in his tracks and removed his hat.

"What day is it, lad?"

The boy seemed even more confused by this but, being a boy reminded often to mind his manners answered, "Today? Why, it's Christmas day."

Scrooge was filled with relief, followed by a joy he couldn't contain. The Ghosts of Christmas had done it all in one night. He had his chance to not only make amends, committing to the vow he proposed to Marley, but to begin this very day. And, to begin in earnest.

Scrooge searched in his pockets and found one of his coin purses. "Do you know the butchers in the next street?"

The boy acknowledged that not only did he know them, but that, of course, any boy his age would know his way around the neighborhood.

"A remarkable and intelligent lad. Do you know if they've yet sold the prize turkey?" Scrooge asked, holding his coin purse.

"The big one?" The boy seemed to lose his earlier confusion and was becoming swept up by the excitement the man was radiating. "I just passed them. It looks like it's all prepared for Christmas lunch, but it's still there."

Scrooge leapt excitedly, forgetting his rheumatism for a moment, but was reminded as he landed. "Oh, what joy. Go and buy it."

"What's that?" The boy squawked, putting a hand on his hip.

"My apologies, you were likely on an errand for your mother to be out so early on this day. But if you can go and buy it for me and meet me there in ten minutes, I will give you half a crown for your efforts."

The boy stumbled forward, eager to complete the task Scrooge had assigned. He raised his hands up as Scrooge tossed his money purse down and caught it deftly before it could get lost in the snow, immediately taking off like a sharp shot down the alley toward the butcher shop.

Scrooge hadn't had as agreeable an interaction with a child since Fred was a lad. What struck him more forcefully than that realization, was how he hadn't worried if the money might become lost in the snow. He had been overcome by the boy's tenacity to complete the job and by his own excitement for whom the Christmas lunch was for.

Scrooge paused in front of the looking glass on his way back to the bedchamber to dress for Christmas day for the first time in many years. He studied himself for just a moment, noting the smile he hadn't realized he wore.

He only had a few minutes before he should be at the butcher's place. He cleaned up quickly and put on his best clothing fit for a day of celebration and happiness. Coming into his sitting room, he regarded the two chairs. Looking at Marley's he felt a heaviness in his chest. All this time, he thought the chair was empty, but now he knew better.

"Jacob? Wherever you are. Whether it was all a dream or was real is of no matter now, but know that it has changed me. I will remember the zest for life you carried. I am sorry I forgot." He didn't cry this time, though he knew he was far from having shed all the tears he had within. "I love you, Jacob. And, as I have been shown this night, I know now that I can love you even more by sharing it with others around me." He pulled out the pocket watch, polishing the inscription with his dry thumb. "I must go and wish everyone I encounter a Happy Christmas. I suppose I'll surprise some people in the process."

He sobered as he imagined people's faces as they opened their doors to find him on the other side. He worried they may not believe his transformation or react kindly to him, and he reasoned they would only be right to treat him as he had them.

With no time to be too bothered about the possible reactions to his changed nature, Scrooge rushed out and was at the butcher's before he even felt the cold. The warmth radiating within him and a bidding of Christmas wish to each and every soul he passed kept him buoyant and effervescent in his task. The butcher was wary of the boy at first, thinking he was putting him on, but was more than happy to be proven wrong after Scrooge arrived and paid almost twice what the bird was worth to have it delivered to the Cratchit home immediately.

He then paid the boy and before Scrooge bid him farewell, he told him that he would need a smart courier, as he would have quite a bit of upcoming work delivering many messages of paid debts and forgiven loans. Scrooge asked the lad to come by for work, should he be interested. The boy expressed his agreement and was off even faster than before, to prove to Scrooge he would be a diligent and proficient errand boy. Scrooge grinned as he watched the boy run, puffs of fresh snow fluffing in his wake.

For once, Scrooge didn't know what to do with himself. He was too early for celebrations at his nephew's house. So, he let himself wander, guided by the spirit of the moment. He wished a Happy Christmas to everyone he passed, garnering confused stares from those who recognized him.

As he passed the Exchange, he waved down two businessmen he recognized from his visit with the Ghost of Christmas Future. He shook each of their hands and wished them well…and was, in turn, met with skeptical looks. He explained, he understood they may think his change of heart peculiar, and that he wouldn't have been surprised were any of them calling for him to be escorted to Bedlam. They nodded and smiled a little at that, returning short response of well-wishes to him.

Scrooge was soon overcome with the pleasure of the moment. He outlined an offer for them to partner with him on a new business opportunity, one he was sure would be worth their while. They wondered all the more that they shouldn't take him to the authorities. Scrooge knew they may be suspicious, but if any of them took him up on the offer, he would hold true to his promise and that would be enough to ensure others would follow.

He bid them farewell and Happy Christmas again, hoping they had been equally moved by the interaction. He hoped it might even spur them to forgive any prior grievance they may hold against him or Marley.

"I am happy to do it for us, Jacob." He whispered and then realized there was a place he really had to be.

He hurried to the residence of the Wilkins family. Upon knocking on the door, he was greeted by the housemaid who showed him in, as the lady of the house was awake and prepping for festivities.

Scrooge was asked to wait in the parlor, but after a moment, walked directly to the drawing room. It hadn't changed from those midnight moments with the ghosts, nor had it changed much from the last time he was there as an invited guest. He regarded the mantel and the debonair, cutting figure of his partner Marley.

"He was always handsome."

Scrooge turned to see Belle standing in the doorway, her arms hugging herself. His normal walls of defense nearly instantly melted away. He crossed the room with a quickness that rivaled his new courier boy. Grasping the shocked woman in a tight embrace, he offered a million apologies for how everything happened, whispered how much he loved Marley, and how he wished they could have been around her more. And, while he knew it would take some time, he wanted to make amends.

Belle slumped deeper into the embrace with each acknowledgement of her own sadness. She held the man tightly and accepted his apologies, as she knew he was sincere. She, too, asked for forgiveness for her role in how they had parted, explaining that she never meant to expose their secret, but that it had become quite normal for her to think of the two of them together as they complimented and brightened each other's lives so well. She knew her brother was never happier than after he had met Scrooge.

She bid they sit in front of the fire and rekindle the friendship they once had. The maid brought them a tray of breakfast breads and strong tea, to which Scrooge expressed his gratitude for her kindness, not feeling he was owed anything given how he was now showing up quite unannounced.

Once properly alone, Scrooge held her hand and, looking at his love's portrait, confessed he had tried to fool himself into thinking she'd done it on purpose. Assigning her ill intent made it easier to stay resentful and suspicious towards her and everyone else. But he and Marley never really believed she was intentionally at fault for their being discovered.

"Jacob would, every once in a while, be overcome by a sadness. He never said what was bothering him. But I know he missed you." He explained they both missed her fiercely, but didn't know how to fix what had unraveled. Scrooge hung his head. Belle squeezed his hand. "And especially after his passing, I was only able to see the horrible side of humanity."

Belle cleared her throat and patted Scrooge's hand. "I always knew my brother was different. And I loved him for it." Rising she went to the mantel. Scrooge watched in wonder, unsure what she might say next. He took a timid sip of tea and put the cup back down on the saucer with a clink. She turned to face him. "It fills me with such joy to talk with you and about him. I have missed you, Ebby."

"I've missed you, too, Belle," Scrooge said. "I've missed the three of us. After everything happened, it never felt complete when we would walk the Thames or sit in the park just the two of us," Scrooge reflected, and then laughed. "We missed you. You were more than a chaperone. You were my friend."

She nodded and smiled at him. "You will always be welcome here. I would love for you to meet Jacob's nephews and their children. I want them to know who their uncle was, and you would be able to help me do his memory justice."

Scrooge promised he would, but asked forgiveness for needing to take his leave as he felt it only prudent he not interrupt her Christmas morning any further.

Next time he would come by announced and, with him, bring many stories and remembrances of his beloved.

She invited him to a New Year's lunch, to which he was only ecstatic to oblige and felt a lightheartedness he forgot he could experience at the mere thought of having plans to meet for a family dinner.

"Thank you, Belle. I'll be there."

She tilted her head, studying Scrooge. "Ebby?" Again, that name he hadn't heard in many years, chipping away at what was left of the walls around his heart. "Please tell me this is a permanent change. You seem so much more like the you I used to know."

To which, Scrooge could only nod.

"I will have this sent over to your apartment." She pointed at the painting of Marley. "It never should have left." And at that, tears sprung forth, tears he was no longer embarrassed to shed. She took his reaction as agreement to her suggestion and, dabbing her own eyes with her handkerchief, showed him to the door where they embraced one last time before Scrooge exited.

He collected himself as he returned to the sidewalk. He was overcome with relief at how easy that had been to talk with Belle and scolded himself a bit for his foolishness in thinking it wouldn't have gone as well as it had. Of course she would be sad to lose them both, he had been too. He thanked the Ghost of Christmas Present for showing him her sadness, noting they had it in common.

With a cleansing breath, he continued on, still unsure where he was headed. Idly he navigated the roads he knew by heart, eventually walking past the Old Bailey. Knowing it was Christmas in there, too, he shouted so the prisoners might hear the sound of someone wishing them a good day.

His joyous demeanor faltered as the realization dawned of where he'd unconsciously but, perhaps intentionally, ended up. He heaved a sigh and continued on to the church and into its adjacent graveyard.

He entered through the gate, and into a calm, cold, and desolate place. He had only been one other time and that had been at night. But his memory was strong. Scrooge was able to wind his way through the paths to the grave marker of Jacob Marley. It was spartan in appearance, compared to the ones around it. It gave him no joy to be standing there, except that he wanted to be in the light and honor his love without worrying others would see.

Even though he hadn't worn it in years, Scrooge fingered the pocket watch to offer him some comfort. He shook his head to clear the memory of Old Joe and Mrs. Dilber chittering over his possessions. That was the future he intended to avoid.

He bowed his head, saying a silent prayer he knew from his childhood, and felt he had finally completed an obligation he had long ignored. He committed to visit more frequently, even as he realized Marley could as easily be sitting in his chair at home. He felt comforted by the knowledge no one could keep him from visiting.

Scrooge heaved a sigh of relief as he exited the graveyard from the other gated entrance and crossed the street to a business he knew would be open. He expected that the laundress who owed him money would be at her wash table and that was where he found her. Her breath caught in her chest at the appearance of the man at her business.

"Ya linens're done Misser Scrooge, but I adn't wish to disturb ya today. And as far as the money I owes, I'll be needin' more time." She then rattled off a litany of griefs, from the illnesses of her mother and youngest daughter to the imprisonment of her husband for something which he hadn't done, but for which he was somehow responsible.

"I'm not here for money, my good lady." He smiled hoping this gesture would show his sincerity. "I was in the neighborhood and thought I would pick up my delivery. Save you the trouble of coming over to my house."

The woman scrunched her face in astonished puzzlement. "Aye, they're 'ere sir." She turned to bring them as quick as she could. She was bothered by his presence, and his smile, and wanted to be rid of him more than she wanted her curiosity satisfied, this man who haunted her every decision. He was, after all, the reason she was working on Christmas, instead of with her two children attempting rest and joy on this day.

When she returned, Scrooge produced a payment that was four-fold her normal fee. Her eyes bulged at the sum of money sitting on the neatly packaged pile of washing.

"I assure you, your work deserves more. And the only way to properly compensate you for the many years of your diligent service is to forgive the rest of your debt as well."

The laundress clutched her chest, fearing her heart would stop. Between the overpayment and the forgiveness of debt she would be able to pay off her husband's bail and release him from prison. She gaped, unable to form words.

Her response had an immediate effect on Scrooge. He could see his action had provided for her and her family, and he realized you could keep a business alive by creating bonds with people out of kindness and love. And perhaps, those ties were stronger, and longer lasting, than those forged from fear.

"I think you must 'ave gone mad?" She kept placing her hand on her breast and then her forehead. She was breathing very quickly. "Sorry, Misser Scrooge, 'at wasn't very kind."

Scrooge chortled. "I am not sure. But I do know that I *had* lost my senses, and hopefully now have come to find them." He pushed the tower of linens with his payment atop towards her. "I do have someplace to be now, so I will have my courier pick these up tomorrow. You should close up and have a Christmas with your family."

"I will, sir." She still could not quite believe all that had transpired but, she was beginning to accept that it was reality. "And a Happy Christmas to you as well."

He stopped on the threshold and turned back to face her. "If you have any trouble with the barrister or local constable, let me know, and I'll see what I can do to help your husband."

She lunged forward grabbing his arm, and through the tears, gushed a string of thank-yous and God-Save-Yous.

He held her hand and thanked her for her kind wishes just as the rear door opened and, who would walk in, but Mrs. Dilber. Anger flashed across her face as she tried to work out why Scrooge was bothering this establishment. "Eh, 'ere now? What's he doing t'ya?"

Scrooge chuckled. "I assure you, Mrs. Dilber, I am only doing what I should have done many years ago for her and for you, too." He then expressed his gratitude for her service over the many years and humbly apologized for making her work miserable and especially on Christmas. He promptly presented her a sum of money equal to what he had given the laundress. Mrs. Dilber could not recover from her shock, mouth hanging open as she took the large sum of money in her hand and stared at it as if it were the rarest jewel on Earth.

The laundress was overcome and thanked him again, finally bidding him farewell. To which he replied, "A Happy Christmas to you both." As he took his leave, he wondered to himself if Mrs. Dilber's mouth could have opened any wider in her astonishment.

The laundress' shop was just the first stop on his repentance tour. He paid a visit to a few more shop owners and peddlers, surprising them with similar payments and well-wishes before finding himself on his nephew's street. His good humor nearly evaporated as the church bells tolled three o'clock and the reality of facing what might come next sunk in.

Scrooge stood, pensively looking up at the home. He thought how fun it would be to surprise them, but realized it was equally likely they would be unwilling to let him in.

But, if he were invited in, to enjoy pudding and spirits with the crowd before retiring for the night, it would make a good start at setting things right.

Scrooge had to knock more than twice to get a response at the door. Likely the housemaid had been given the day off, and he was glad all over again that he hadn't made Cratchit appear at work this morning. Twas the lady of the house, his niece-in-law, Clara, who answered the door. Her face, delightfully red and cheery, slackened at the visage of the character standing on her doorstep. With eyes as large as Christmas wreaths, she regarded the man to whom she hadn't ever been properly introduced.

"I say!" Clara finally blurted after a few moments pause. She was a beautiful young woman, with a gentle nature, in which Scrooge could immediately identify the movements and intimations of his sister. His heart felt heavy at all the missed opportunities to spend time with them.

Scrooge's shoulders slumped. "My dear niece, can you ever find it in your heart to forgive me. I have squandered all the joy we may have experienced as a family. Might you let this old fool come in?"

She remained dumbstruck, but stepped back, and with a gesture of her hand, offered him entrance to their home. "Can I take your coat please?" She came more to herself after realizing the momentous occasion this was. Fred had only just finished a toast praying his uncle would have a changed nature. With a reflective sigh and a smile, wondering if this really was a Christmas miracle, she helped her uncle out of his over clothes. "We had lunch, but I could make up a plate if you're hungry."

Scrooge took a deep breath. "No, thank you, my dear. Right now, I must see my nephew. They would all be in there, playing games?" Scrooge pushed the door open a crack allowing the sounds of the party filter out to them.

"But...how would you know that?" Clara whispered, frozen, rooted to the spot, holding his coat.

Scrooge smiled back at her and then turned to enter the room. As he had predicted, at this very moment they were in the middle of a game of Blindman's Bluff. He first noticed his nephew's back, shaking with silent laughter, as he backed away from the seeker, and almost directly into Scrooge. The blindfolded partygoer continued around the room away from them.

Fred stood taller, as he was now safe, and he adjusted his waistcoat. He looked behind him to see if his wife had returned, at first looking past Scrooge, before, with a jolt of amazement, returning his gaze to his uncle. He blinked many times before opening his mouth with an astonished inhale. "You came?" A few others around them gaped and gasped at the presence of the lonely miser.

Scrooge put a finger to his lips and motioned toward the man with the blindfold who was having a very difficult time finding anyone, but had located them with Fred's exclamation. Fred wasn't concerned about the game any longer and pulled his uncle towards him in an embrace Scrooge was more than happy to enter. He cried for a second time that day and offered a quiet confession of his sorrow, as Fred shushed him, telling him there was no need for any apologies today. The greatest gift was that he was there. Scrooge let go of Fred as the blindfolded man reached out, touching Scrooge's shoulder.

"Ahhh. Now I have found someone. I thought you had all walked out of the room." He turned his covered head back and forth, mouth smiling full of teeth. Scrooge tried to remain silent but couldn't prevent a laugh from escaping. The astonished partygoers around him realized Scrooge was enjoying himself, and they too started to chuckle along.

"I can tell who this is right away." The blindfolded man patted Scrooge's chest and shoulders, his ears, and the top of his head. He now wore a frown instead of a smile, which only made Scrooge laugh harder. The man cocked his head forward, "But dear me, that's a laugh I don't think I've ever heard before." The rest of the crowd cheerfully agreed, laughing along with Scrooge at the man's puzzlement.

"You only get one guess." Clara called from the drawing room door.

"Yes, only one." Fred agreed.

The man shook his head. "Is it Pip? No wait. It's Oliver." The two men named laughed heartily from their places around the room, confirming he was incorrect, as the rest of the crowd joined in a chorus of nays.

He removed the blindfold to see that he was holding on to the shoulder of the last person he would have guessed to be at the party. "Ebeneezer?"

"Charles Darcy. We meet this time under better circumstances. And me, very glad you didn't guess correctly."

He smiled and shook his head. "Well, I see I have been played the fool. Do you think it's been all these years you've told everyone you hated Christmas, all so this year your nephew would finally be able to say I didn't win a round of this game?"

The crowd erupted in raucous chatter and laughter at the suggestion.

Scrooge leaned towards him, with an ashamed look and a sober tone. "Charles, we should meet soon to discuss the many back-payments Scrooge and Marley owe the foundation you have established."

Darcy was surprised, even more than seeing him here, to hear Scrooge offer to donate money. "Yes." He clapped a hand to Scrooge's shoulder, pulling him into a tight embrace. "Over a meal and drink some time we can discuss it. And remember a man we both dearly cared about."

Scrooge, ever capable of surprise himself, blushed and nodded. "I would like that. Over dinner we will talk donations."

"And over drinks we will reminisce as old friends." Darcy grabbed a glass off the tray Clara was bringing around and handed it to Scrooge. Fred and Clara held glasses high and toasted everyone's health.

Scrooge felt overcome by their acceptance of him, relieved at how he worried they could have reacted. He felt tears prick again at his eyes, but they were tears of happiness rather than regret or sadness.

He added to the toast, "And God bless us everyone."

The evening was a success. Everyone left well-fed and happy. Scrooge talked with everyone, wishing them all well and blessings for the Christmas season and the New Year. He got to talk more with Darcy and felt a rejuvenation of a friendship he once knew. He and Fred reminisced about the generosity and kindness of Fred's mother and Scrooge noted how much Clara seemed just like her. By the time Scrooge left, he had said goodbye to all the other departing guests and had even had a second helping of Christmas pudding.

Rising early the next morning, Scrooge couldn't recall the last time he was nervous to go to work. He prepped and dressed with a quickness and left his chambers after a small breakfast of porridge, making sure to eat something substantial as Marley might be watching. He arrived at his office well before the hour he expected Cratchit, only to find his new errand boy patiently standing at the door.

"See here sir. I'm as good as me word." The boy beamed as Scrooge opened the office for the day.

Scrooge wasted no time in getting him to his tasks and sent him off on three errands. First and foremost, to the laundress. "And be sure to let every one of them know I mean every word in the letter." And then he halted, thinking they may worry he was collecting on their debts after all. "Well, my boy, say that to them after they read my letter."

He opened the door for the lad and watched him take off in the snow. Still a little time before Cratchit arrived. Scrooge began to pace and practice aloud how he would tell Cratchit about his new promotion and salary adjustment. He would have looked mad to anyone watching, had they stopped to look inside the Scrooge and Marley offices.

The door opened, and Scrooge had to compose himself quickly. But it was his errand boy, returned with his linens already. He placed them neatly on the bench by the door and crossed the room to hand Scrooge an envelope.

"What's this?" Scrooge looked down at the lad.

The boy shrugged. "It's from the Laundress. She told me to hand it only t'you and not open it or read it. If I did, you'd turn back into an angry old scratch." Scrooge looked down at his newest employee, bewildered by his courage to say such a thing to him, and yet, realized it was probably true.

The boy for his part, bowed his head, grasping his cap tighter. "Was her words, I'm only repeatin', sir. Don't need to shout at me." The boy averted his eyes to the floor.

Scrooge harrumphed and plucked the envelope from the boy's outstretched hand. It was thoroughly sealed and, upon opening it fully, he saw a slip a hastily written note alongside a much older looking envelope. Scrooge didn't know what to make of these items.

Dear Sir,

Your kindness will never be truly thanked. I can only say my family will be forever grateful. Even Mrs. Dilber agrees we hope your nature is true. We decided to return this item to you.

It was the evidence that confirmed it. Although, we were pretty sure something was going on when there was only ever one set of linens to wash from you and Mister Marley's chambers.

Scrooge regarded the other envelope and, opening the back, recognized Jacob Marley's handwriting. "I thought I'd lost it." It was the first love letter he had ever received from anyone. He blinked back tears, as he placed the letter in his coat pocket. His eyes widened as realization came to him. She was the one who had led to his downfall in that future he prayed he would avoid. It was not a fellow businessman, but rather someone indebted to him. Scrooge continued reading her note.

It never felt right anyway, and I cannot excuse my reasons for keeping it in my possession. Me and Mrs. Dilber talked about it all the time, wanting to make you see how wicked you treated us, those of us who did everything for you. Excuse me for saying so now, sir.

It's beautiful what he says to you. I wish my husband would say things so lovely. I think it was what stopped me. If someone in this world could love you that much, maybe you weren't so bad.

"You ok, sir?" The boy seemed genuinely concerned about Scrooge.

Scrooge nodded. "Better now than even yesterday. And here you are with your work for the day done already. I would still pay you a full day's worth."

He gave the boy his wages and he was happy to run home with a promise to return the following day. Scrooge bid him farewell and Happy Christmas.

Scrooge returned to his desk, permitting his tears to flow freely now as he read Marley's words from many years ago. When he finished, he held the letter to his chest allowing the feeling of love to embrace him. He felt a new life breathing into him and made a resolution to keep this feeling of love all year round.

He looked at Marley's empty desk chair. "I think we may have done it, my love. I think we might just be safe now." He sobered as he heard the front door clatter open.

Cratchit entered and threw off his coat clumsily before adjusting his chair with many a scratching and scraping sound. Scrooge waited until the ruckus died down, knowing Cratchit would be settled in his chair and attempting to engage in his work.

"Cratchit." Scrooge worked hard to sound as menacing and disappointed as he could, hiding his nerves like a trained stage performer. But felt he could never be this angry at anyone again, especially his loyal employee.

Cratchit's chair scraped back slowly, and, after a few timid steps, he appeared at the door. "Yes, sir?"

"You're late." Scrooge remained seated. "Come here." He pointed to the area next to the desks he and Marley had shared.

"I know, Mr. Scrooge and I apologize deeply. There was so much to do..." Cratchit massaged his hands and blew into them to keep warm, afraid his employer would finally dismiss him from his position. And on Boxing Day, at that. At least he would be able to help his wife and children carry their collection home from the church.

"Enough." Scrooge interrupted him. "I don't pay you good money to be lazy after a family meal of Christmas turkey."

The thought of his family transformed Cratchit's fear into resolve and he was ready to finally defend himself but was caught off guard when Scrooge jumped out of this chair.

"Was there enough for Tim to get his fill?" The old man, no longer able to keep up the charade hopped toward the stunned man.

Cratchit could have been pushed over by the slightest exhale Scrooge released. His mouth dropped open and his eyes grew large enough they risked falling out of his head all together. Scrooge chuckled and smiled, moving to his colleague's side.

Cratchit, astonished, continued fumbling, "That was...Thank you sir...I wouldn't have guessed...We thought it was someone from the church...but...it was...Oh, thank you," all the while shaking Scrooge's hand with such vigor it threatened to dislodge from his wrist completely.

Scrooge attempted to calm him. "I owe you much more than I could ever pay you. Your loyalty to Jacob and I, and even with my nastiness. I only hope to make it up to you and your family somehow."

Cratchit's face fell, saddened. "I know it's been hard on you losing Mister Marley. I miss him too, actually."

Scrooge patted the man on the back. "And I know Jacob would agree with me and my choice for who will be my next business partner." Scrooge gestured to Marley's Desk. "I think here is the best place for you now."

Cratchit could hardly believe what he was hearing. Lightheaded at the mention of a partnership, and the obvious raise in his wages that would provide, he sat down in Marley's chair to keep from landing face first on the floor.

"Why is it always so cold in here? Bob, throw another heap of coal on the fire and join me." He laughed good-naturedly at Cratchit, feeling a little like the Ghost of Christmas Present. Scrooge produced a dusty bottle of dark liquor from which the two men drank, toasting to a new year, happiness, and many more blessings.

Scrooge was as good as his word and, in fact, infinitely better. He met with Charles Darcy and partnered with his foundation, providing for the poor and abandoned souls of the city, becoming almost like a second father to the unfortunate and cast-out members of society. After promoting Cratchit to partner, he offered to help Tim achieve all his scholarly dreams by sponsoring him at a select boarding school where he might meet more boys interested in the same things as him. Tim was ecstatic and referred to Scrooge as "uncle" from then on.

Finding he quite liked being an uncle, he attended his nephew's annual Christmas lunch - and many lunches in between - after also making a tradition of Christmas breakfast tea with Belle at her home. The painting of her brother was now forever on display above Scrooge's fireplace, and he was never seen without his glimmering pocket watch.

There were, of course, those that laughed at his change of heart and thought it to be a farce or, perhaps,

a new business tactic, as while he was now generous of
spirit, he was still shrewd in his business dealings.

His new driving purpose, however, was that he
might make better lives for the peoples his prior
business acts affected. He expected the gossip around
him to turn nasty.

But he was surprised that many more turned up to
do business with him and witness for themselves the
kindness and joy the man emanated. He found himself
surrounded by a surprising number of loyal friends and
defenders, who would argue that he was a man of the
highest moral principle and utmost generosity to anyone
that disagreed, none more vehemently than the
laundress and Mrs. Dilber. Scrooge learned that love
and generosity created more loyalty than fear could.

He wasn't again plagued by a night of ghosts, except for
on his very last. On a future Christmas Eve, in his
bedroom surrounded by loved ones, and not the wake
of vultures which he was certain he had once been
destined. Feeling the finger of death upon him, Scrooge
opened his eyes one final time expecting to see the
pitch-black cloak of the Ghost of Christmas Future.

Instead, Jacob Marley, illuminated by the light of
the roaring fire, standing young and proud and, oh so
handsome, entered the room from the doorway.
Scrooge gasped a small, surprised sound as Marley
reached an unfettered hand forward taking his love's
hand tight. And together, they departed.

ABOUT THE AUTHOR

Jay R. Swanson is a writer and nurse practitioner working in New York City. His published work includes a narrative non-fiction short story, a book chapter in an instructional handbook, several white papers and published research articles for which he was the lead investigator. With two decades of nursing experience Jay has witnessed the triumphs and tragedies of what it means to be a human. He uses writing to escape the realities of his world; crafting spaces where justice doesn't always mean a happy ending, but where love always wins. Jay lives with his spouse happily ever after in Manhattan.

Find more about him and the crafting of this story at
www.jayrswanson.com